THE BATTLE OF IDENTITY

AGAINST MIND, BLOOD AND WORLD

SWAPNIL SRIVASTAV

Contents

Prologue

02 April 2011,
"Dhoni finishes off in style. A magnificent strike into the crowd. India lift the World Cup after 28 years."
- Ravi Shastri

I sprinted towards Vedant's house, my heart racing with excitement. The entire neighborhood was buzzing with the sounds of joy and celebration. It felt like the whole place had come alive. Mr. Shukla was sitting on his old scooter, happily handing out laddus from a large box. He was doing it in such a generous way that it looked like he was distributing Bholenath's prasad. Nearby, Hari, Goli, and Adnan were lighting firecrackers nonstop, making such a racket that it seemed like they might set the entire street on fire.

Then there was Khan Chacha—unlike everyone else, he didn't look too pleased. He was holding a bat in his hand and running after Adnan, yelling at him as if he was really going to hit him this time. Adnan, of course, just laughed and kept running, but the sight of Chacha chasing him was pretty funny.

As soon as I reached Vedant's house, I spotted Mr. Sharma stepping out onto the balcony. He was a large, heavy-set man, his belly stretching against his shirt, and he moved slowly as if each step required effort. He held a box of sweets in one hand, his face beaming with pride. When he saw me, he smiled warmly and handed me a sweet without saying much.

As I took the sweet from him, I glanced up at the balcony, hoping to catch a glimpse of Ved. But he was nowhere to be seen. Without waiting a second, I dashed inside the house and ran straight towards Ved's room, eager to find him.

When I reached the door, I called out, 'Ved!'

But as I entered the room, I saw Ved was sitting on the bed with his legs bent awkwardly. He was staring at the TV with a look of complete shock, as if he were a statue frozen in time.

"Hey, Ved!" I shouted, breathless and exhilarated. "Did you see that six? Dhoni is a legend!"

Vedant's eyes sparkled, his face lit with a joy I'd never seen before. He nodded, speechless, as the reality of India's victory sank in.

That night, I saw something different in Vedant's eyes. India had won the cricket World Cup after 28 long years. Dhoni's incredible six had fulfilled the dreams of 125 crore Indians. Our joy was beyond measure. Everything seemed to be in motion, nothing was static, except for one thing: VEDANT.

Cricket in India is more than just a sport; it's a religion, the most followed sport of the nation. Every little child on the streets knows the rules to play and has dreamed at least once of playing for India.

Dreams sometimes define the whole life of an individual. They are the fire that pushes one towards betterment and victory, ignited by the smallest spark.

The victory of the Indian cricket team was not just a moment of national pride; it was the spark that ignited Vedant's journey - a journey of hard work, passion, and determination.

Vedant, like many children, watched that moment on TV and had a thought that filled him with absolute belief. He trusted that he would do something similar one day. "Dreams" is such a beautiful word for a child. Back then, he didn't care whether his future plans would come true or not. In the end, dreams are like that. They don't always align with reality, but they hold a special place in our hearts. They carry us forward, giving us hope and fueling our passion. It was also the start of a story that would define our youth and ultimately, our lives. It was the inception of Vedant's journey, a journey that started with a single, magnificent six and grew into something far greater.

Introduction

The Battle of Identity: Against Mind, Blood, and World is a story about young people balancing their dreams with family expectations, respect over giving up, and staying focused despite distractions. It shows the challenges young individuals face—between family pressures, society's demands, and their own goals.

In this debut novel, Swapnil Srivastav explores how youth struggle with their minds and fight distractions to focus on what truly matters. The story highlights how important it is to choose dreams over following what others expect and to gain respect by staying true to yourself.

Youth is the most energetic and important phase of life. It's the time to decide what truly matters and prioritize your own goals over what society expects. Our sense of identity is often shaped by what others say, but it's more than that—it's about chasing dreams, embracing responsibility, and taking pride in what you do.

For any nation's future, young people must know who they truly are, stand up for themselves, and inspire others by breaking away from societal norms.

As Mahatma Gandhi once said, *"Be the change that you wish to see in the world."*

Enjoy the read, and may this story inspire you to reflect on your own dreams, priorities, and battles.

Happy Reading.

CHAPTER ONE

THE DREAM

*05 January 2020 Gomti Nagar,
Lucknow, Uttar Pradesh*

"Mummy, hurry up with the breakfast! We're getting late for the match," Vedant called out.

Vedant Sharma, a 15-year-old, skinny and average-height boy. His thin face matched his lean frame. His skin was mostly fair except for his arms, neck, and face, which were tanned brown. The reason was obvious: cricket.

"Coming!" Rima Aunty responded loudly as she came out of the kitchen, balancing two plates of breakfast, one in each hand. Each plate seemed to have a couple of golden- brown parathas and a glass of milk.

The advantage of having an Indian mom is that you can always count on having food ready, even if you're leaving the house at 5 o'clock in the morning.

5

Mrs. Sharma, a proper Indian housewife, moved with practiced ease. Her saree was neatly draped, and her hair was tied back in a bun. The smell of freshly cooked parathas filled the air as she made her way towards Me and Vedant. Her face, always warm and welcoming, showed a hint of hurry as she juggled the tasks of the morning.

As soon as we picked up the first morsel for breakfast, a loud voice echoed from outside, a familiar sound that resonated through the morning air. "Is Doctor Sharma at home?"

Rima Aunty, in her haste, left a half-cooked paratha on the hot griddle and hurried outside in a flurry. "You've come at just the right time, Mr. Shukla. Let's have tea," she said cheerfully.

Mr. Shukla, our neighbor whose house was conveniently located between Vedant's and mine, had just returned from his morning jog. His T-shirt was soaked with sweat, and his forehead was wrinkled with the worry of shedding his belly fat, which he was diligently trying to run off every morning. He stepped in with a wide grin, his eyes twinkling with a hint of mischief. "Where is Santosh?" he asked.

"He's still sleeping," Rima Aunty replied with a calm smile. "Please, have a seat and join us for tea."

"Well, if you insist," Mr. Shukla said, settling himself at the table. As he noticed us in our white cricket kits, he asked, "So, Vedant, how's your cricket going?"

"It's going great, Uncle," Vedant replied enthusiastically, his eyes lighting up. "We have an important match today."

"Good, good," Mr. Shukla said, nodding. "But remember, it's important to balance everything. Your studies are just as important as cricket, if not more."

Vedant nodded, his excitement slightly dampened by the

reminder. Mr. Shukla then turned to me and asked, "Is Srivastav ji at home? I need to discuss something about the market with him."

"No, Uncle," I replied. "Daddy has been out of town for two days. He should be back tonight."

"These businessmen have all the fun, always getting to travel," Mr. Shukla said with a hint of sarcasm, his smile widening as he spoke. He glanced around the room, his eyes searching for someone. "Where's Radhika? I haven't seen her. She's usually so disciplined and sharp. Hasn't she woken up yet?"

Rima Aunty laughed softly, shaking her head. "Radhika's already up, Mr. Shukla. She's gone to the library for her early morning study session. This is her 12th grade, you know how dedicated she is."

Mr. Shukla turned back at Vedant with a smirk. "And you have your board exams this year too, right? 10th grade, isn't it?"

"Yes, Uncle," Vedant responded quietly.

Mr. Shukla casually asked Ved, "Which subjects are you taking in intermediate?" Without thinking much, Ved replied, "Science." Neighbors often ask such questions out of curiosity!

Mr. Shukla raised an eyebrow. "Why take Science if all you want to do is play cricket, Vedant? Why not take Arts like your sister?"

I jumped in before Vedant could respond. "Uncle, he's taking Science because of me. Our school doesn't offer Arts, and my dad wants me to pursue Engineering, so I'm taking Science. Ved and I want to study together."

Mr. Shukla laughed sarcastically. "Huh? Sacrificing your future just to stay together? What a pair of duffers."

Suddenly, a commanding voice cut through the air. "Shukla, don't you dare say a word against my Ved!"

Dadi emerged from her room, holding a basket of flowers and a pot of milk, ready for her morning prayers to Lord Shiva. Clad in a plain white saree. Ved's grandmother and our favorite, Dadi, could tolerate anything said about her late husband but never a word against her grandson or her deity.

"My Ved is doing far better than your Nikku, at least he's not getting his legs broken in a car accident," Dadi retorted sharply.

Mr. Shukla's face turned red but he remained silent, taking a sip of his tea instead. Nikku, Mr. Shukla's son, had recently been in an accident.

Ved and I exchanged a quick smile. Indian parents never miss an opportunity to taunt, and Dadi was the best at it. Probably because of her experiences.

"I think we are getting late," Vedant said to me. We quickly finished our breakfast, bowed to touch Dadi's feet for blessings, and left for the match, determined and ready.

Today was the U-16 trial match. It was extremely important for Ved, though not as much for me, probably because I didn't have the same passion. Maybe I say that because Ved plays much better than I do. As for me, figuring out what I wanted to do in life wasn't a priority. Perhaps because I never faced any difficulties; I came from a wealthy family, and it showed in my physique too. I'm not talking about height - that's genetic, and at 15, I hoped I'd still grow taller. I was fairer than Ved and probably luckier too because I didn't have to worry about my future. I was the only heir to my family's wealth, just as my father had been lucky too, thanks to my grandfather's hard work. My dad was an IIT graduate, so taking Science in 11th grade wasn't just a plan—it was practically a family ritual. Ved's

dad wasn't an IITian, but he was a doctor, which is why Ved is going to take Science too. The only difference is that I'll choose Maths, and he will opt for Biology.

"Ved, stop!" I shouted.

Ved abruptly braked his scooty. "What happened?"

"A cat crossed our path."

"I'll hit a century today," Ved said confidently and drove on.

The morning sun bathed Blaze Ground in a warm glow, casting long shadows that danced across the field in Gomti Nagar, Lucknow. It was 7:00 AM, and the semi-final match of the Interclub Cricket Championship between RCA and DCA was about to begin.

Our spirits were high as we exchanged confident glances, ready to take on the challenge ahead. We had prepared hard for this moment, but as the first innings progressed, it became clear that the day was not going to be an easy one for us. After the first inning, we had to chase 266 runs in 35 overs.

"I told you, a cat crossed our path, we should have stopped," I said to Ved angrily. Maybe I said it because I had given away 49 runs in my six overs without taking a single wicket. Ved didn't respond, perhaps because he was the most upset. As a captain, it's heartbreaking when your team doesn't perform well. Vedant was our captain and wicketkeeper. Now all eyes onto our batting innings. Ravi and Kushagra were set to open our inning.

"Stay there!" Ved said to Ravi.

"If we play to win, we get another chance to showcase our skills in the final, increasing our chances of making the U- 16 team," Ved said to Kushagra.

Still, I trusted the cat that crossed our path more than Ved's words because Kushagra got out on the very first ball.

Even while thinking all this, I said to Ved, "All the best, Ved," as he went onto the field to bat.

I thought today was just going to be a bad day, but my friend Vedant was in a completely different mood. I swear, if he hadn't gotten out today, the match would have been ours.

"What a game you played, Ved! Congrats on being named Man of the Match!" I said, trying to lift his spirits.

Despite his incredible 119 runs, Ved wasn't celebrating. We had lost the match by 11 runs, and it weighed heavily on him.

"I blew it," Ved muttered, frustration lacing his voice. "I had a chance to prove myself in the final, and now I'm worried about my selection, I can't believe we lost," he grumbled, shaking his head. How could I mess up so badly? Ved was very stubborn and never accepted defeat. That might be why he kept growing—he never gave up and always worked hard to improve.

As we made our way home, the weight of the semi-final loss hung over us. The streets were unusually quiet, and our minds were filled with thoughts of what could have been. Ved, still grappling with his disappointment, was silent for most of the ride.

We were in a bad mood after losing the match, but both Ved and I knew that he would be selected since he had scored 119 runs and was the highest run-scorer of the tournament.

"Despite the loss weighing on him, I knew Ved would bounce back quickly. He had that stubborn resilience. So when we reached Hanuman Chowk, I suggested, 'Let's park at Khan Chacha's shop. A cold drink might help lift your spirits—after all, your selection is almost guaranteed.'"

Khan Chacha's general store stood on the right side of Hanuman Chowk, nestled right beside Raza Masjid.

"As we neared Khan Chacha's store, we expected the usual quiet. But today was different. A large crowd gathered in front, their murmurs growing louder as we approached." There was never this much hustle around his store normally. Ved turned to me in surprise and asked, "What could Khan Chacha be selling today to attract such a crowd?"

As we approached the shop, we found that Khan Chacha wasn't there. Instead, Adnan, his son, was behind the counter.

"Ved glanced at Adnan behind the counter, his voice uncertain. 'Where's Chacha?' Adnan hesitated, his eyes shifting nervously. 'He... he's in the next alley, bhaiya... but...' 'But what?' I asked, sensing something was wrong. Before Adnan could respond, an older man nearby broke the silence. 'Siddiqui's daughter... she took poison. She's gone.'"

"Yes, Abba has gone there," Adnan said. "Siddiqui's daughter! Fatima?" Ved asked in shock. "Yes, that's right. Uncle replied."

"Ved's face went pale. 'Fatima? Radhika didi's classmate?' I could barely process it myself. 'And Amir's sister,' I whispered, my heart sinking. Amir had no idea yet—my dad had taken him out for work, blissfully unaware of the storm brewing at home."

"As we reached Amir's house, the air was thick with murmurs. Clusters of neighbors stood in tense conversation, their faces somber. Every whisper, every word seemed to revolve around one thing—Fatima."

"Rumors drifted through the crowd like poison itself. One man muttered that Siddiqui had beaten Fatima regularly.

My heart sank—could that be true? I'd never imagined things were so bad."

"Ever since Siddiqui's wife ran away, he had become a very short-tempered man. He would beat his daughter every day. The poor girl couldn't take it anymore, so she took poison," an old uncle said.

"Others blamed Vikki Chaturvedi, the younger brother of MLA Seenu Chaturvedi. 'He harassed her,' they whispered. The rumors swirled, each more alarming than the last, leaving me dizzy with uncertainty. Which version was true? Who could I believe?" Vikki Chaturvedi was the younger brother of Seenu Chaturvedi, who was the MLA of the Lucknow East constituency.

I was utterly confused, unable to determine which of the rumors were true. My mind was racing, but all I could think about was Amir, he had no idea what was happening. "My heart raced, the weight of uncertainty pressing down on me. I fumbled for my phone, hands trembling as I dialed Dad's number. Each ring felt like an eternity, my breath catching in my throat. I needed to hear his voice, to know that Amir was okay." When he finally answered, I hurriedly explained the situation, my voice shaky with concern. "Dad listened in silence as I poured out the frantic details, my words spilling over each other. When I finally paused, his voice came through steady, a calm in the storm. 'I know,' he said softly. 'I've heard what happened. Don't worry, I'm with Amir—we're on our way back now.'" "Though Dad's words eased the immediate panic, the knot in my stomach remained tight. The air around us still buzzed with tension, with questions, with rumors. All I could do was wait—wait for Amir to return, wait for the truth to surface."

Amir has always been like a younger brother to me. "I can still picture the day Amir first arrived at our home, small and wide-eyed, clutching his mother's Burqa like it was the only anchor in a world he didn't understand. He barely spoke, and when he did, it was in a whisper, as though afraid his voice might betray his uncertainty." Ever since that day, Amir has been living with us. Now, he's in the 8th grade, attending the same school as me, and despite the years that have passed, it still feels like he just became part of our family. Whenever Dad goes out of town, he always takes Amir along, as if he were his own son.

His mother used to work as a maid in our house, but one day she just left. She didn't tell anyone where she was going or why, and since then, Amir stayed with us. "Her departure left a silence that we all quietly accepted, and Amir became a part of our family without ever needing to explain why. But now, with Fatima gone, the quiet around

Amir has deepened into something far more painful." He knew where his real home was, though. He often visited Mr. Siddiqui and Fatima, but he never really spoke about his mother, not to me, not to anyone.

"Now, with Fatima gone, I can barely grasp the storm of grief that must be raging inside Amir. His mother abandoned him, and now his sister—the only other tether to his past—has been ripped away from him. How does a boy his age make sense of that kind of loss?" The thought keeps tearing at me.

We waited until the evening. Fatima's body hadn't been taken to the cemetery yet, and the atmosphere was thick with grief and exhaustion. People sat around in silence, murmuring prayers, waiting for Amir. Finally, he arrived, with Dad by his side. As soon as he stepped out of the car, I could see the anguish on his face. He didn't hesitate for a second. He rushed to Fatima's body, collapsing beside her, crying as though the weight of the world had fallen on his small shoulders. Mr. Siddiqui held him close, the two of them wrapped in each other's sorrow, weeping together in the stillness of the evening.

Ved and I exchanged a glance, not knowing what to say or do. We walked over to Dad, who looked at us with tired eyes and simply said, "You both head home. I'll stay with Mr. Siddiqui for a while and come back later."

That night, sitting alone in my room, I couldn't stop thinking about Amir. Ved and I were busy worrying about making the cricket team, but Amir—who was younger than both of us—was facing something far more unbearable. His life had been shattered, piece by piece.

Abandoned by his mother, and now grieving the loss of his sister, he had a father who barely cared for him. I kept wondering what was going through his mind—whether he was questioning life itself, or if he even had the strength to keep going. The more I thought about it, the more I realized how insignificant our own worries seemed compared to what Amir must be feeling. "The pain and loneliness Amir must be feeling... it was unfathomable, a darkness I couldn't even begin to touch. And yet, it haunted me, creeping into my thoughts and weighing on my heart, long after the world outside had gone quiet."

The door creaked open softly.

"Son, you're still awake?" Dad's voice was soft, though I could hear the quiet worry threading through his tone.

I turned toward the doorway and saw him standing there, silhouetted in the dim light. "Dad..."

"You haven't slept yet?" he asked, stepping into the room.

I hesitated, then asked, "Where's Amir, Dad?" My worry hung in the air, impossible to hide.

"Amir's at home," Dad replied, his tone soft but steady. "Mr. Siddiqui needs him right now."

I nodded, trying to make sense of everything that had happened today. The weight of it all felt too heavy.

"Dad walked to the chair and sat down, loosening his tie, as if the weight of the day clung to him too. For a moment, he stayed silent, then, in his usual steady way, asked, 'So, tell me, how was the match?' It felt jarring, like a shift too sudden, but Dad had a way of knowing when to distract me, even when my thoughts were elsewhere."

"I looked away, trying to shake off the weight pressing on my chest. 'We lost,' I muttered. It felt wrong to even care about the match when Amir's world was falling apart, but somehow, the sting of losing still lingered."

Dad didn't rush me. He waited a moment, then asked gently, "How did you play?"

I sighed, knowing I couldn't hide the truth. "I gave away 49 runs in 6 overs."

"Wickets?" he pressed, his tone still calm.

"I shook my head, the disappointment heavy in my chest. 'None.' Each ball I bowled felt like it slipped right out of my control, and by the end, I could barely look my teammates in the eye."

Dad leaned back in the chair, nodding thoughtfully. He wasn't the type to lecture or make me feel worse. Instead, he asked, "Was the pitch tough? Not turning, or maybe too much grass?"

"The pitch wasn't bad... but the batsmen were," I admitted. "The other team... they were just better."

"And Vedant? How did he do?"

At the mention of Vedant, my mood lifted a little. "He was incredible, Dad. Scored 119 runs."

Dad raised his eyebrows in surprise. "And still, you lost?" "Just by 11 runs," I said, my voice dropping again.

He paused for a moment, then asked the question I'd been dreading. "What went wrong?"

I hesitated, knowing how ridiculous it sounded. "On the way to the ground this morning, a cat crossed our path." My voice was barely above a whisper, but the embarrassment lingered.

"'Ah, that old nonsense!' Dad laughed, a warm sound that felt out of place in the heaviness of the moment. 'Your mother used to believe in all those superstitions too.' His gaze flicked toward her photo, draped in marigolds, a soft fondness in his eyes. 'She'd tell you, stay up too late, and you'll have nightmares for days.'"

I don't know how true that was, but while we were talking, the date had already changed. So, Dad ordered me to go to bed since I had to go to school the next morning.

No matter how painful a situation might be, if it doesn't directly affect you, it doesn't take long to forget. "Morning came too soon, pulling me out of the thoughts that had kept me awake long after Dad left my room. School beckoned, with its usual noise and rush, but as Ved and I walked through the gates, the weight of last night still clung to me, refusing to fade." The usual chatter and laughter were replaced with a palpable tension. The atmosphere was charged, and it wasn't long before we realized why—every corner of the school was buzzing with just one topic: the Board Exams. In India, even the smallest issues can spark endless discussions, but this was a significant matter for every student, a looming challenge that couldn't be ignored.

But I didn't really care—not because I wasn't interested in studying. On the contrary, I was quite studious, likely inheriting that trait from my father. Yet, despite my dedication to academics, I never felt the burning desire to top the class, even though it happened often enough. My focus wasn't on outshining everyone else; I was content with simply understanding the material and doing well.

The atmosphere in our classroom was a mix of anxiety and anticipation, perfectly reflecting the significance of our 10th-grade year. It was a turning point for all of us, a time when we were on the brink of making decisions that would shape our futures. Some of my friends were already planning to take up arts and prepare for civil service exams, following in the footsteps of people like Radhika Didi. Others were deep in discussions about careers in medicine, debating the best coaching centers and study materials.

Ved was part of those conversations, sitting quietly among them. I couldn't help but notice the contrast between his silent participation and the enthusiasm of those around him. It made me smile, knowing full well that he had no real interest in becoming a doctor. His heart was elsewhere, in a world where stethoscopes and scalpel sets held no allure. When our eyes met, he smiled back, a silent acknowledgment between us. We both knew where his true passion lay—on the cricket field, not in a hospital ward. It was only a matter of time before he would join the U-16 cricket team, a dream that was far more real and exciting for him than any medical career could ever be.

Meanwhile, some of our classmates were already deep in discussions about which coaching institutes to choose for engineering entrance exams. I found myself drawn to those conversations, as I, too, was planning to head down that path. In our country, the lives of young people are incredibly challenging, particularly when it comes to making decisions that could determine the course of our futures. Perhaps it's because we are often reminded that we are the future of the nation, which is why it is so challenging.

To make it easier, our school announced that starting in the 11th grade, classes would be divided: one section for engineering aspirants and another for those pursuing medical studies. The goal was clear—help students focus on their specific paths, making the grueling journey just a bit easier.

As soon as the announcement was made, Ved and I exchanged worried glances. It felt like the school didn't care about our friendship at all. We had been through so much together, and the idea of being separated, even just by different classes, was unsettling. We both wanted to oppose this decision, to stand up for the bond we had, but it quickly became apparent that most of our classmates supported the change. For them, preparing for the entrance exams had become more important than anything else, even friendships.

In a moment of frustration, I was about to suggest to Ved that we switch schools in the 11th grade. But as I opened my mouth to speak, I hesitated. The reality of the situation hit me—the entrance exams were crucial for me. My own ambitions, the drive to succeed, momentarily overshadowed the importance of our friendship, making me pause and reconsider.

I turned to Ved, forcing a casual tone. "So, what do you think?"

I half-expected him to suggest we leave and find a new school together. But he didn't. Maybe he saw how important these exams were to me. Maybe he didn't want to burden me with more decisions. Instead, he gave a small, knowing smile and said, *"At least we'll still go to and come back from school together."*

His words, simple yet profound, grounded me. It was a quiet acceptance of the change, a reminder that while our paths might diverge, our friendship would remain.

I grinned and said, "You're definitely going to make the U- 16 team."

"I know," he replied with that same quiet confidence I admired in him.

A few days later, the much-anticipated day finally arrived— the day when the State Under-16 team would be announced. Ved had been in top form throughout the tournament, and his performance had been nothing short of extraordinary. He had consistently outshone the competition, emerging as the highest run-scorer. We were both anxious but excited, knowing that his hard work had put him in a strong position.

"Today was the day the team list would be released, and we were eagerly waiting for it to arrive on our phones. The tension was palpable, each moment feeling like an eternity as we checked our screens."

The team announcement was scheduled for 9 AM sharp, but before that, Ved's father, Mr. Sharma, developed an insatiable craving for jalebi. Now, when Mr. Sharma gets a craving, it's not something you ignore. So, without further ado, we found ourselves at Ramu Bhaiya's shop, watching as the golden, syrupy coils of jalebi sizzled in hot oil.

"'Sunday is such a perfect day,' I mused aloud, as the sweet smell of jalebis filled the air, almost enough to distract me from the tension gnawing in my stomach."

"We were heading home, still riding the small joy of our jalebi hunt, when Ved suddenly froze. 'Oh no, we forgot the dahi!' he exclaimed, and I couldn't help but laugh. In the Sharma household, jalebis without curd was a culinary crime."

Now, if you're unfamiliar with the peculiar culinary traditions of the Sharma household, let me enlighten you. Ved's father had this unshakeable belief that the sweetness of jalebi had to be balanced by the tanginess of curd.

According to him, eating them together was not only delicious but also somehow balanced the universe—or at least your digestive system. Whether or not there was any truth to this theory, we didn't dare challenge it. So, back we went to fetch the curd, laughing at ourselves the whole way.

On our return, just as we were about to enter the house, we were intercepted by Mr. Shukla, our ever-curious neighbor. He stood on his porch, hands on his hips, a bemused expression on his face as he watched us with the curd in one hand and jalebis in the other.

"Where are you two off to so early in the morning?" he asked, eyebrows raised in mock suspicion.

"Uncle, we just went out to get some jalebi," Ved explained, holding up the packet as evidence. "Why don't you join us for breakfast?"

Mr. Shukla's curiosity melted into a smile, and soon enough, the Sharma family, Mr. Shukla, and I were all seated together at the breakfast table, ready to dive into a feast of jalebi and curd. The hall was filled with the sound of laughter and clinking plates as we prepared to indulge in the treat.

"Just as I was about to pop a piece of jalebi into my mouth, my phone buzzed with a notification. My heart skipped a beat. The time had come—8:59 AM. In an instant, the warmth of the moment vanished, replaced by the cold rush of reality." I shot a glance at Ved, and I could see the same mix of panic and anticipation in his eyes. In a flurry of motion, we both put our jalebis back on the plate, forgetting all about breakfast as we frantically grabbed our phones.

I fumbled to unlock my phone, my fingers suddenly feeling clumsy, and tapped on the notification. The screen seemed to take forever to load, and each passing second felt like an eternity. Finally, the list of selected players appeared before my eyes.

"As I scanned the names, the excitement drained from me like air escaping a punctured balloon. The names of the selected wicketkeepers—Shubham Patel and Vikki Chaturvedi—stared back at me, mocking the expectation that had filled the morning."

I couldn't believe it. Ved had been the highest run-scorer in the entire tournament and was the best wicketkeeper by far. How could he not have made the team? I looked over at Ved, my mind struggling to process what had just happened.

Ved's face, which had been so full of excitement just moments ago, now wore an expression of deep disappointment. The spark in his eyes had dimmed, replaced by a look of quiet resignation. It was as if the confident, determined boy I knew had been momentarily replaced by someone grappling with a bitter reality. The sight was heartbreaking, and for a moment, the world around us seemed to go silent, leaving only the sting of this unexpected defeat hanging in the air. The expression in Ved's eyes now was so different from the hopeful and determined look I had seen nine years ago.

CHAPTER TWO

AMIR

"Ved! Ved! Wake up, man!" I shouted, my voice tinged with urgency, but there was no response from the other side of the door.

I knocked louder, frustration creeping in. "Come on, Ved, it's time for practice! We're going to be late if you don't get up now. Who sleeps in the evening? Get up, buddy!"

But the silence that followed only deepened my concern. It wasn't just that Ved was still in bed; something didn't feel right. My heart began to race as I knocked again, this time with more force. "Ved, come on, you need to open the door!" I called again, my voice cracking slightly.

Silence.

The door finally creaked open. His face—

He looked nothing like the energetic guy I knew. His hair was tousled, his brow furrowed, and his eyes were heavy with exhaustion. There was a seriousness in his expression that sent a chill down my spine.

"I'm not sure I'm up for it today," he mumbled, his voice low and strained, as if it took all his energy just to speak. He avoided making eye contact, instead staring down at the floor, his shoulders slumped under the weight of something I couldn't quite grasp.

It was as if the fire that usually burned so brightly in him had been reduced to a flicker. I could sense that this wasn't just about being tired or needing more sleep. There was something deeper going on, something that had sapped the life out of him. My worry grew even stronger, and I knew I couldn't just leave him like this.

"Ved," I said, softer this time, "What's going on?" I softened my voice, stepping closer. "Talk to me, man..."

He finally looked up at me, and in his eyes, I saw a mix of frustration, doubt, and something that looked a lot like fear. It was a look I had never seen in him before, and it made my chest tighten. This wasn't just about skipping practice. Ved was struggling with something much bigger.

I walked into the room, gently closing the door behind me, as if I didn't want to disturb the fragile silence. The room was cloaked in darkness, the heavy curtains drawn tightly across the windows, blocking out any hint of sunlight. The atmosphere was thick with gloom, the kind that wraps around you and refuses to let go. I scanned the room, my eyes landing on Vedant's bed—a chaotic mess of crumpled sheets and pillows scattered haphazardly, as if they'd been through a stormy night of tossing and turning.

"Ved," I began softly, trying to break through the dense fog of despair that seemed to have settled in, "I know you're feeling down about not making the U-16 team, but you're a fighter. Hiding out in here won't change anything. You need to face it head-on and figure out what comes next." I paused, trying to inject some humor to lighten the mood. "And honestly, man, I've never known anyone as stubbornly egoistic as you. You've never backed down from anything, so how did you end up in this pit of self-pity?"

Ved sighed heavily, the sound echoing in the dim room as he slumped down on the edge of the bed, looking as though he was carrying the weight of the world on his shoulders. His expression was a mix of frustration and exhaustion, like he'd been wrestling with his thoughts all day. "I've been pushing so hard," he said, his voice thick with emotion, "but it feels like I'm just slamming into a brick wall every time."

I couldn't resist adding a bit of dramatic wisdom, trying to stir the fighter in him. "Hey, don't let this knock you off your game. Even the greatest heroes face their share of challenges and setbacks. You're on the path to becoming one of those heroes, Ved. *It's not about how many times you fall, but how you pick yourself up after each fall.*"

He looked up at me, and for a brief moment, I saw a flicker of the old Ved—determined, resilient, and ready to take on the world. But the flicker was faint, as if it was struggling to stay alive. *"It's just... hard to keep going sometimes,"* he admitted, his voice barely above a whisper, as though saying it out loud made it all too real.

Before I could respond, the door creaked open slowly, and in walked Dadi, her steps light but filled with purpose. She was wrapped in her favorite shawl, the one she always wore on chilly evenings, and it gave her an aura of warmth and reassurance. Even in the dim light, her presence seemed to brighten the room, like a comforting glow in the midst of all the darkness.

"What's all this noise about?" she asked, her voice soft yet commanding, the kind that could soothe a storm but also demand answers. She looked at both of us, her eyes twinkling with a mix of concern and gentle reprimand.

I couldn't help but smile at the sight of her. Dadi had this magical ability to step into a room and instantly make everything seem less dire. Even when things felt like they were falling apart, she could put it all back together with just a few wise words and a comforting pat on the back.

"Dadi," I said, trying to sound as casual as possible, "we're just having a little talk here, trying to figure out how to get Ved back on his feet."

She nodded, as if she already knew everything without needing an explanation. "Well, my boys, sometimes it takes a little fall to remind you of the strength you have to get back up," she said, her words carrying the weight of years of wisdom. "But don't stay down too long. *Life's too short to spend it sulking in the dark.*"

Ved looked at her, and for the first time since I walked in, a small smile tugged at the corners of his mouth.

It was clear that Dadi's presence was having an effect, bringing a bit of light into the room that had been so full of shadows just moments before.

As Dadi settled into a chair near the bed, wrapping her shawl more tightly around her, I felt a sense of relief wash over me. With her here, I knew that whatever Ved was going through, he wasn't going to be facing it alone. And with that thought, the darkness in the room didn't seem so overwhelming anymore.

I gave Ved a friendly nudge, trying to lift his spirits. "Come on, Ved! Even Dadi's rooting for you. And if that's not enough, I promise to get you your favorite pakoras after practice."

Ved looked up at me, and for the time, I saw a flicker of determination in his eyes. A hint of a smile began to tug at the corners of his lips, like a reluctant sunrise breaking through a stormy sky. "Alright, alright," he said, his voice carrying a note of resolve. "I'll come."

As we left his room together, I could see that Ved was beginning to shake off the shadows that had settled over him. The familiar surroundings of the house seemed to offer a bit of comfort and normalcy, and Dadi's encouragement had clearly done its part. Sometimes, all it takes is the right kind of motivation and the support of those who believe in you to reignite the fire within.

We were just about to head out when we heard Radhika didi's voice calling from behind us. "Hey, are you taking the church route to the ground? I need to grab some books from the stationery shop. Can I come along?"

Vedant gave me a mischievous grin and said, "No, you can't."

I immediately jumped in with a grin of my own, "Of course she can."

At that moment, Mr. Sharma's booming voice came from inside the house, sounding like he had just put down a half- eaten samosa to make his point. "Riding with three people is illegal, don't you know?"

Vedant shot back with a cheeky smile, *"It's totally fine, Papa. We're in India. Even if it's illegal, it feels legal."*

Mr. Sharma's voice grew even louder, filled with mock seriousness. "If the traffic police catch you, I'm not paying the fine."

Radhika didi, never one to back down, shouted from the doorway, "I'll pay it!" She said this with a dramatic flair that made it clear she was determined to join us. "Now, let's go!"

Mr. Sharma's voice echoed from inside, mixing frustration with a hint of humor. "And where are you going to get the money from?"

As Vedant started the scooty, the conversation turned into a lively debate with lots of laughter and teasing. With Mr. Sharma's warnings fading into the background, we set off down the road, ready to tackle the adventures, fines or no fines.

The evening in Gomti Nagar was a portrait of calm amidst the usual city chaos. As the bikes, rickshaws, and cars whizzed by, the cool breeze swept through, turning the hectic noise into a distant murmur. It was as if the wind had a magical power to smooth over the clamor of the day, transforming it into a peaceful retreat. The rustling leaves, the occasional distant chatter, and the soft hum of the evening created a soothing symphony, making it feel like the city itself was taking a deep, relaxing breath.

We rode along the serene streets, each of us soaking in the tranquility. The cool evening air had a way of turning even the busiest of streets into a haven of calm. The usual cacophony of the city seemed to be on vacation, replaced by a gentle, almost ethereal quiet. It was like nature's way of reminding us that even in the heart of urban life, moments of peace and simplicity were always within reach.

"What a beautiful evening!" I said, my voice filled with the awe of the moment. I took a deep breath, savoring the refreshing breeze as if it were a rare treat.

"It really is," Radhika didi agreed, her smile mirroring the contentment in her voice.

Ved, always the realist, added with a playful smirk, "Let's just hope we don't run into any traffic police. We wouldn't want this perfect evening to be spoiled by a ticket."

As if on cue, the streets were blissfully free of traffic officers. It seemed even the traffic police were enjoying the evening off, soaking up the pleasant weather and leaving the roads a little emptier for us. It was as though everyone—cars, bikes, rickshaws, and even the traffic enforcers— had collectively decided to embrace the serenity of the evening, making the roads feel like a private lane just for us.

We chuckled at the thought, appreciating how the city's usual bustle had been momentarily replaced by a peaceful calm. It was a delightful reminder that amidst the constant rush, there were always pockets of tranquility waiting to be discovered, even if it meant a bit of humor to complete the experience.

When we reached the stationery shop, it looked like the entire neighborhood had decided to skip their evening tea and gather for an impromptu drama session. People weren't there for the usual notebooks or pens; something far more interesting had caught their attention. In India, it doesn't take much for a crowd to form—a heated argument, a cow blocking traffic, or, in this case, something that seemed much juicier.

As we approached, I noticed the crowd wasn't just gathered for a casual chat. No, this was a full-on scolding session, and the unfortunate star of the show was a boy being held by the collar.

"Amir!" I yelled as soon as I spotted him, smack in the middle of the crowd, looking like a deer caught in the headlights. And holding onto him like he was trying to squeeze the truth out of a lemon was none other than Vikki Chaturvedi, our local trouble magnet.

Without thinking, I pushed through the crowd—because in situations like these, thinking is for later—and pulled Amir away from Vikki's iron grip. "What's going on, Amir?" I asked, but Amir was too busy impersonating a goldfish to answer—his mouth opened and closed, but no words came out.

"Chor saala!" Vikki hollered, pointing a finger at Amir like he'd just caught him stealing the nation's supply of jalebis. The crowd gasped, as if they were watching the climax of a Bollywood movie.

I tried to get some clarity, but Vikki was too busy seething to offer any explanations. "This bastard is the son of that wretched Siddiqui!" Vikki snarled, as if that was supposed to explain everything. "Tell your father he won't be spared!" He delivered the line with the kind of dramatic flair that would make any soap opera villain proud.

Before I could get a word in, Vikki stormed off like he had a date with destiny, or maybe just dinner. He hopped into his black Thar with the swagger of a guy who thinks he just delivered a mic drop moment. With a roar of the engine, he sped off, leaving the crowd to disperse and us to pick up the pieces.

Ved and I guided Amir over to the scooty, both of us trying to make sense of what had just happened. I looked at Amir, concern etched on my face, and asked, "Amir, what's going on? It's been ten days since you've been home. Dad said you wanted to spend some time at your own place with Mr. Siddiqui, so I didn't press you. But I was planning to check in on you after practice today. So, what happened? And why was Vikki attacking you like that?"

Amir took a deep breath, clearly shaken, but trying his best to maintain composure. "Bhaiya..." he began, his voice quivering slightly as he tried to steady himself. He held up a book—*Dr. Abdul Kalam's autobiography, Wings of Fire.* "I just came here to buy this book. But when Vikki saw me, he called me over. He started saying awful things about Abba, so I... I couldn't take it and I cursed him back. That's when he started hitting me."

"Why was he badmouthing Abba?" I asked, my voice tinged with concern.

"I don't know, Bhaiya. I really don't know," Amir replied, his confusion and hurt evident in his tone.

Radhika Didi, who had been quietly listening, suddenly spoke up, her frustration clear. "He used to say horrible things about Fatima too! Once, he even came into the classroom and insulted her in front of everyone. I got into a fight with him back then. If he had stayed a little longer today, *Bholenath ki kasam,* I wouldn't have let him go so easily!" she fumed, her anger bubbling to the surface as she recalled the incident.

I looked Amir straight in the eye and said, "You're coming home with me. No arguments."

"Bhaiya, Abba will be alone," Amir replied, his voice filled with concern.

"And what about your studies? The Physics book in my drawer is missing you. You haven't been to school in days!" I shot back.

Amir was just as passionate about studying as I was. The way Ved loved cricket, I had that same love for Physics. Studying for the pure love of it is something very few people understand, and Amir was one of those rare souls who shared my passion for Physics.

"Yes, bhaiya, I'll go to school from tomorrow," Amir promised, looking like a kid caught with his hand in the cookie jar.

I raised an eyebrow, giving him my best "older brother knows best" look. "You know, books won't read themselves, and trust me, they won't be happy about it either. And you don't want to break Newton's heart, do you?"

Amir chuckled, shaking his head. "No, Bhaiya, I wouldn't want that."

"Good," I said, patting him on the back. "And remember, you and I need to stay ahead in the brain race. I can't let Ved steal all the glory with his cricket skills."

"Radhika didi said she'd drop Amir off after picking up her books. 'You two go ahead to practice,' she added."

CHAPTER THREE

EXAMINOPHOBIA

When I finally made it back home from practice, I headed straight to my room. The sight of my 10th-grade textbook on the desk felt like a betrayal. It used to be a companion, but now it seemed like a symbol of all the things I'd neglected. I'd always been the type who actually liked studying, but lately, my books had become the equivalent of that one plant you forget to water. It wasn't my usual style to slack off, but with Amir missing and no one to study with, I'd developed a sudden aversion to textbooks.

I sat on the edge of my bed, glaring at the book as if it had personally betrayed me. I wanted to dive into it and catch up on everything I'd missed, but my body felt like it had been hit by a ton of bricks. I leaned back and stared at the ceiling, trying to muster the energy to get up. The ceiling, however, wasn't much of a motivational speaker.

Just then, I heard the housemaid's voice through the door. "Baba, Saheb is calling."

"Coming," I replied, my voice betraying how utterly exhausted I was.

With great effort, I dragged myself out of bed and shuffled to Dad's room. The room was bathed in the gentle, soothing glow of a bedside lamp, creating a cozy, almost nostalgic ambiance. Dad was lounging on the bed, looking relaxed and deeply thoughtful, his diary and pen resting in his hands. He seemed lost in his own world, possibly plotting world domination or, more likely, just jotting down his reflections.

"How was your day?" he asked, his tone calm and steady, as though he was prepared for anything.

I took in the serene atmosphere of the room before filling him in on the drama with Amir and Vikki. Dad listened intently, nodding at the appropriate moments, and once I was done, he leaned back, his expression turning more contemplative.

Then, with a mischievous glint in his eye, he revealed a secret that would make any soap opera jealous. He told me that Mr. Siddiqui's wife was actually a Hindu woman. I nearly choked on my own surprise. And to add another twist to this unfolding drama, she was the maternal sister of Seenu Chaturvedi. It was like discovering that your favorite TV show had just added a plot twist you didn't see coming. I sat there, dumbfounded, realizing that our small town was practically bursting with hidden stories and secrets, and I'd just stumbled upon one of the juiciest ones yet.

"Wait a minute," I said, eyes popping like I'd just seen a ghost. "So, you're telling me Vikki is Amir's Mama? I knew family gatherings could be awkward, but this is next level!"

"Yeah, that's right," Dad said, nodding gravely. "But let's put a pin in the family drama for now. I called you in here because—" he glanced at me with a touch of concern

—"your exam is coming up in a few days, right?" He shifted on the bed, leaning slightly on his elbows, and set aside his diary and pen as if to give me his full, undivided attention.

"Yes," I replied, my voice tinged with the dawning realization of how little time I had left to prepare.

"Alright then," Dad said, eyeing me with a mix of paternal concern and curiosity. "How's the study marathon going?"

I hesitated for a moment, feeling the gravity of his question. It was like he'd just asked me to confess to a secret crime. I appreciated his concern, but let's face it—I hadn't exactly been hitting the books with the dedication of a study-obsessed hermit. "Well," I said, trying to sound like I had it all under control, "I've been studying all year, except, you know, for the last few days. But I'm sure I'll pull through."

Dad gave me one of those thoughtful looks that made me feel like he was channeling some deep philosophical wisdom. "You know," he began, *"sometimes we get so caught up in doing things we love—like, say, binge- watching a series or perfecting your cricket swing—that we forget about what really matters. Time slips away like a mischievous gremlin, and once it's gone, it's not coming back. Distractions are sneaky devils, but it's important to remember our responsibilities and priorities. Balance your passions with your duties, or you might find yourself regretting the lost opportunities. Time is like a relentless river—it keeps flowing whether we're paddling or not."*

Dad leaned back on his bed, a twinkle of nostalgia in his eyes. "You know," he said, his voice carrying a blend of pride and mischief, "I was the only kid in my school who managed to crack the IIT exam on my first try. Your principal might have mentioned it—he was my teacher back then."

I nodded, remembering the day our principal had mentioned Dad's achievement in front of the entire class. "Yes, he did," I said with a chuckle. "He spoke about it with such enthusiasm, it was like he was trying to turn you into a school legend. It was quite the proud moment for me to hear that."

Dad's smile widened, clearly enjoying the trip down memory lane. "Want to know the secret to my success on that first attempt?" he asked, leaning in as if he was about to reveal the formula for the perfect cup of coffee.

"You were just incredibly smart and dedicated," I guessed, trying to match his playful tone.

"Obviously, being good at studies is a major factor—you can't crack an exam like IIT without putting in the effort. It's about more than just natural ability; it's about practice and a genuine interest in the subject."

He paused for a moment, letting his words sink in, before adding with a grin, "But you know what the most important reason was?"

I raised an eyebrow, curious. "What's that?"

With a playful glint in his eye, Dad said, *"I wanted to impress your mother."*

I couldn't help but laugh. "So, that's why you two got engaged? Trying to impress Mom was a big part of your motivation?"

Dad's smile widened. "Just one of the reasons. Let's say it added a little extra spice to the mix."

As I listened, a lightbulb went off in my head. "You know, *maybe aiming to impress your crush instead of just focusing on beating other students can be a powerful motivator in exams.*"

Dad chuckled, clearly pleased with the thought. "Exactly. When you have a personal reason driving you, it can make all the difference."

"That's... that's great!" I said, feeling a new sense of motivation.

"Indeed, it was," Dad replied, his tone reflecting the satisfaction of a lesson well learned.

Dad shifted his tone to something more contemplative, the kind of serious that makes you sit up straighter. "You know, *the true measure of success,*" he began, "*isn't about how you stack up against others. It's really about how well you achieve the priorities you set for yourself. It's not a* competition with everyone else—it's about staying true to your own goals and values."

He paused, as if letting the weight of his words settle in. Then, with a thoughtful expression, he asked, "If Vedant were to top his board exams but didn't make the under-19 cricket team, do you think he'd be happy or sad?"

"Probably sad," I ventured, unsure where this was leading.

"Exactly!" Dad said, nodding vigorously. "Because his priority is cricket. Now, let me turn the tables. If you were in the same situation—failing your exams but getting selected for the under-19 team—would you be happy?"

I mulled it over, trying to picture myself in that scenario. "Ahhh... no," I finally said, "I'd probably be pretty upset."

"Right!" Dad said, with a knowing smile. "Because, while you enjoy studying and excel at it, losing out on something you deeply care about is tough. Your priority right now is your studies, isn't it? Do you get where I'm coming from?"

"Yeah, Dad," I nodded, finally catching on.

Dad leaned back, looking quite satisfied with his mini-lecture. "Remember, enjoyments are temporary. You can always dive into cricket later. For now, focus on what's important."

I couldn't help but think that sometimes parents are like GPS devices—they give great directions, but they might not always be perfect. "It's true that you should listen to your parents; they're often the best advisors. But sometimes, they might not have all the answers. Like, take Mr. Siddiqui, for example. I don't think he'd be much help advising Amir. In fact, it looks like he might need advice himself, rather than dishing it out."

That night, after Dad's story had left me both amused and inspired, I found myself giving my physics books a long, lingering look. It was as if I was about to go on a date with them—romantic candlelight dinner style, except it was my desk lamp illuminating the pages and not a flickering candle. I cracked open the book with the same excitement one might approach a long-lost love, ready to dive into the world of equations and theories with newfound enthusiasm.

Dad's words had rekindled my passion for studying, turning my usual reluctance into eager anticipation. The books seemed to whisper promises of academic adventure, and I was ready to embrace every moment of it, as if each page turned was another step closer to achieving my own goals.

The next day, Sunday, was perfect for a student. The evening was peaceful, with a gentle breeze rustling through Ved's garden, where a lively game of cricket was in full swing.

Ved was clearly upset. "Out!" he shouted, his frustration obvious.

"No, it's a no ball," Radhika didi countered firmly.

"It's not a no ball; it's a clean out!" Ved insisted, his face growing red with anger.

"It's above my waist, so it's a no ball," Radhika didi said, standing her ground.

"No way! You're cheating!" Ved snapped back.

In the middle of this heated exchange, Radhika didi turned to me. "You decide—was that a fair ball?"

I hesitated, feeling the pressure of the moment. "Um... it's... a no ball," I said, not entirely sure of my stance.

Just then, Amir appeared at the garden gate and spoke up with surprising authority, "It was a fair ball. That's out."

His sudden intervention brought an immediate silence. Everyone turned to Amir, who had arrived just in time to end the debate. His decisive words settled the argument, and the game resumed with a new sense of order, proving that sometimes, a timely comment is all it takes to calm things down.

After the match—Vedant, of course, came out on top, as usual—we all flopped down on the couch, still riding the high from the game. The conversation naturally drifted to our upcoming board exams, a topic that was lurking in the back of all our minds.

The atmosphere was light, filled with the lingering energy of friendly competition. Dadi, who had been quietly observing us from her favorite chair, suddenly perked up. As we chatted, she leaned in, her eyes twinkling with interest. Every now and then, she would nod sagely, throwing in a nugget of wisdom or two about her own school days—which, according to her, were the golden years of education.

Her involvement added a cozy layer to the moment, like a warm blanket on a cold day. It was clear that, despite the generation gap, Dadi was just as invested in our academic futures as we were. Her presence turned what could have been a stressful discussion about exams into a family moment, complete with laughter, a few good-natured jabs, and more than a little nostalgia.

Radhika didi was casually bragging about how the UPSC is her real target and the 12th board exams are just a laddoo for her—easy peasy. And honestly, she's got the creds to say that, having aced her 10th board like a boss. But then there's her little brother, Ved—sweet, charming, and completely allergic to studying. The guy somehow always manages to just pass, and I'm still trying to figure out what kind of magic trick he pulls off every time.

Ved, though, was ridiculously confident. He strutted around like he was too cool for school, convinced he could pass his exams without breaking a sweat. No tutors, no extra help—just pure, unshakable belief that he could breeze through with minimal effort.

Meanwhile, Amir was bubbling with excitement about his own board exams, still two years away. But Ved quickly burst his bubble, saying, *"Dude, it's all just hype. Don't get your hopes up. The real thrill is sweating it out on the cricket field."*

And as for me? Well, I had my own approach. I found comfort in tackling math problems, diving headfirst into physics, and giving chemistry the same level of attention

Ved gave to his textbooks—basically none. It was my survival strategy, and it worked like a charm.

The board exams had descended like a storm, whipping up the usual frenzy among Indian parents, teachers, and every relative within a 500-mile radius. The atmosphere at Vedant's house was electric, buzzing with a mix of anxiety and unsolicited advice. It was like everyone had a PhD in stressing out over exams. Rima Aunty's phone was ringing off the hook, mostly with the same nosy question: "Is the boy studying, or is he still messing around the cricket field?"

Honestly, if I were Vedant, I'd have pretended to study every time the phone rang, just to dodge those questions. But Vedant? Nah. He was the definition of chill, barely glancing at his textbooks. It was as if the looming exams were just a distant rumor, something other kids worried about. I couldn't wrap my head around it—how on earth did he think he was going to pass, let alone ace, these exams with that level of nonchalance?

The only person who had unshakeable faith in Vedant was Dadi. She was convinced he wasn't just going to pass; he was going to top the exams. "Just wait and see," she'd say with unwavering confidence. "With Bhole Baba's blessings, my Ved will top the exams." Every single day, she'd hand him a glass of milk, declaring it as Prasad from Shiv Ji, a divine boost for his brainpower. And Vedant, ever the dutiful grandson, would drink it down, probably hoping that Shiv Ji would take care of the rest while he stuck to his laid-back routine.

The days slipped by faster than a cricket ball in the final over, and before we knew it, the day of reckoning—result day—had arrived.

My result turned out just as I had expected. I knew my papers had gone well, so it wasn't much of a surprise when I saw my name at the top of the list. But honestly, that wasn't the result I was most excited about. All my thoughts were on Ved's result.

When I reached his house, the scene was exactly as I had pictured it: a quiet room filled with a calm, almost icy atmosphere. Ved was sitting next to Dadi on the sofa, looking like a soldier who had just returned from a long battle. Radhika didi and Rima aunty stood nearby, their expressions unreadable. Mr. Sharma was on the other sofa, his small eyebrows raised as he glared at me the moment I walked in. It was the kind of look that could stop a cricket ball mid-air.

Radhika didi gave me a subtle signal not to say anything, then asked, "How's your result?" Sensing the tension in the room, I assumed the worst—that Ved had failed. So, rather than boast about my top rank, I simply smiled and said, "I passed."

As I quietly asked Didi about Ved's result, I was surprised to learn that Ved had passed the exams, but he had only barely managed to get passing marks. He was just on the verge of failing, which explained why Mr. Sharma was so angry. Mr. Sharma had really hoped that Ved would at least score well in his board exams, especially because he wanted Ved to pursue a career in the medical field. The tension in the room was palpable.

I was about to congratulate him. However, I stopped myself, realizing that this wasn't the right moment.

"I don't think you're going to play cricket anymore," Mr. Sharma said in a serious tone, his voice cutting through the silence. Ved looked down, clearly affected by his father's disappointment. The atmosphere in the room grew even colder, and I could sense the weight of Mr. Sharma's words pressing down on Ved.

Just when the tension seemed like it might start causing cracks in the walls, Dadi stepped in like a superwoman with her trademark calm. She declared with confidence that Vedant would ace his 12th boards. Her soothing words and faith managed to diffuse the tension, almost like a magical spell.

With the skill of a seasoned negotiator, Dadi also managed to convince Mr. Sharma that cricket and studies were two separate worlds—one didn't affect the other. In a move that felt like a strategic masterstroke, she ensured that Vedant could continue to chase cricket balls without his father's glare shadowing his every swing. It was clear that Dadi knew just how to restore peace, proving once again that sometimes, the most effective solutions come with a side of traditional wisdom and a pinch of tactical charm.

Finally, after all the scolding and lectures, Ved said exactly what I was thinking: "If only I'd opened a book a bit more before the exams."

While we were still discussing it, Amir walked in, all serious in his white kurta and pajama, fresh from Namāz.

Ved and I were trying to figure out what to do next. He'd just barely passed his 10th exams and was supposed to study science now.

Mr. Sharma kept saying, "Sports isn't a reliable career," and honestly, I kind of agreed.

But Ved, with his stubborn grin, said, "If I don't give cricket my best shot, I'll regret it forever. Medical school? No way! I'd rather hold a bat than a syringe any day. So what if I didn't make it to U-16? I'll try for U-19 next."

Amir, always ready with a question, chimed in, "But bhaiya, how did that joker Vikki get selected for U-16? He's decent, but not better than you.

Ved smirked and replied, "His older brother hands out sweets during elections, right? He probably handed out sweets for this selection too."

Just then, Radhika didi came, shaking her head. "One day, I'm going to ban all those sweets," she muttered.

As if the day hadn't been eventful enough, I decided to drop another bombshell. "Ahhh... I've got something to tell you. I'm heading to Kota next week..."

"What? Why?" Ved's eyes widened in surprise. "For preparation," I replied, trying to sound casual.

"Wait, does that mean you're leaving school?" Ved asked, clearly concerned.

"Not really," I said with a shrug. "Dad's got connections— knows the principal and all that. So, I just have to show up for the grand finale—the 12th boards."

"How is that even possible?" Amir jumped in, his eyebrows doing a little dance of disbelief.

I couldn't resist grinning like the cat that got the cream. "Well, I did top the school. So, yeah, it's possible for me."

Ved tried to muster up some enthusiasm. "That's... great,"

he said, but his smile looked like it was about to collapse under the weight of whatever was going on in his head. His eyes, though, were clearly screaming, "Traitor!"

I couldn't help but feel a pang of guilt thinking about leaving Ved to practice alone. The guy was going to miss my perfect bowling and the endless banter. But at that moment, JEE was my top priority. Maybe I was wrong, maybe I wasn't. But right then, it felt like the only thing that mattered. I looked over at Amir and said, "If you need anything, just ask Dad. Although, I'm guessing you're spending more time at the egg shop than hitting the books these days." Mr. Siddiqui has an egg shop, by the way.

I wasn't exactly scared of JEE—okay, maybe a little—but I knew it would be tough. I'd learned from Ved how to enjoy the tough challenges. The next two years were going to be nothing like what I was used to. No more cricket strategies with Vedant, no more political debates with Radhika didi (which I never won anyway), no more physics theories with Amir, and definitely no more chess tactics with Dad.

The morning I was set to leave, Dad looked at me and asked, "All set?"

"Yeah, just a little bit of nervousness," I admitted, gripping the handle of my luggage like it might run off without me.

"I was too when I left home for the first time," Dad said, his voice softening as nostalgia took over.

I hesitated, my anxiety bubbling up. "But what if I don't clear the exam?"

Dad gave me that look—half stern, half comforting, like only dads can. "You've got the brains, My Son. Give it your best for the next two years, and JEE won't stand a chance. And remember, you're heading to Kota to prepare, not just to pass. Focus on the work, and the results will handle themselves."

Then, with a flair for the dramatic, he handed me a chessboard. "And don't forget to practice your tactics. A sharp mind wins battles."

I couldn't resist a dig. "You've never beaten me, not even once," I said, smirking.

Dad's grin widened. "That's because I've always let you win," he said, winking. "But maybe the new city will teach you some new tricks."

CHAPTER FOUR

IAS Abhishek Singh

"Kota, Rajasthan"

The hostel room I was assigned to looked like the scene of a thousand late-night battles with textbooks. The walls had been transformed into a collage of dreams, sweat, and possibly a few tears. As I scanned the room, I felt certain that the previous occupant had either achieved greatness or gone mad trying. The original color of the walls was a mystery, hidden beneath layers of newspaper clippings, study notes, and motivational quotes. After a moment of squinting, I discovered a patch of ceiling that had escaped the academic carnage—it was white.

In front of the door, like a declaration of war, someone had scrawled in bold, black letters: *"IAS Abhishek Singh."* It felt less like a name and more like a battle cry.

The brother who had helped me lug my luggage into the room stuck around for a while, probably sensing that I was a bit overwhelmed by the sheer intensity of the place. As I surveyed the walls, still absorbing the vibe of the previous tenant's relentless dedication, curiosity got the better of me.

I turned to him and asked, "So, where's the person who used to live here?"

He gave me a look like he was about to spill some juicy gossip and leaned in a bit. "Oh, let me tell you," he said, with a grin that suggested I was in for some interesting news. "The prelims results just came out yesterday. The person who stayed here probably cracked the prelims and has now headed off to Delhi to prepare for the mains. That's why this room just became available."

Hearing this news made me feel like I had just won the lottery. The idea that the room I was about to use for my JEE preparation had been home to someone who was on their way to becoming an IAS officer filled me with a mix of pride and motivation. It was as if the room itself had some magical aura of success, and now it was my turn to soak it all in.

My confidence shot up as I started unpacking my belongings, carefully placing my books and clothes in the same space where greatness had clearly thrived. The walls, plastered with notes and motivational quotes, seemed to whisper encouragement to me. I could almost feel the lingering energy of hard work and perseverance, and it made me feel like I was stepping into some big shoes— shoes I was determined to fill.

Once I had settled in, freshened up, and shifted everything to its new home, I sat down to plan my attack on the JEE. As I sketched out my study schedule, I could feel my determination building. The room, with all its history and inspiration, was pushing me to be my best.

Just as I was getting into the zone, deep in thought about how to tackle my first study session, there was a knock on the door.

"Who is it?" I called out, already half-expecting an amusing response.

"It's me," came the reply from outside.

I couldn't help but chuckle to myself. This line was classic Ved. Every time he visited my house, he'd knock on the door, and when I asked who it was, he would always answer, "It's me." It was so predictable that it practically became an inside joke between us. No matter how many times he pulled this stunt, it never failed to make me smile. It was Ved's signature way of announcing his presence—so laid-back, yet so unmistakably him.

So, when I heard that familiar "It's me" this time, I couldn't help but think that whoever was knocking must be cut from the same cloth as Ved. The routine was so similar that I half-expected to see Ved's grinning face on the other side of the door, ready to crack a joke or two.

But as soon as I opened the door, any thoughts of Ved vanished. Instead of his familiar smile, I was greeted by a massive, dark hand reaching out toward me. My eyebrows shot up in surprise, and I tilted my head back to take in the sight before me—a guy who looked like he could bench press a bus. He was easily six feet tall, big and heavy, with a face that looked like it had seen some serious life, complete with an almost fully grown mustache that seemed to have its own personality. His sheer size and tough appearance made me pause, wondering if I was about to be squashed like a bug.

But then, the giant broke into a surprisingly warm smile, introducing himself in a deep, booming voice that seemed to echo down the hallway. "Hriday Tripathy from Odisha," he said. "I'm in class 11th at JIL Institute, preparing for NEET."

"Ahhh... okay," I managed to say, more out of shock than anything else.

Hriday didn't seem to notice my momentary panic and casually continued, "NEET, JEE, or UPSC?"

".... JEE," I replied, still processing the fact that this mountain of a man was standing in front of me.

Turns out, Hriday was my neighbor, living in the room right next to mine. As we continued talking, I found out that he came from a family as impressive as his physique. Hriday has three brothers, and each of them has a story. His eldest brother had tried his hand at UPSC but didn't quite make it; now he's a teacher, probably scaring the life out of his students with just a look. The middle brother, however, had hit the jackpot and was studying engineering at IIT Kharagpur, which made me nod in approval and feel a little spark of happiness—I mean, who wouldn't want a future IITian living next door?

Hriday himself was in Kota preparing for NEET, which made sense given his dedication and serious demeanor. He also mentioned having an elder sister who was married, and a mother who was a retired teacher—a nice, gentle image that was a bit at odds with Hriday's rugged appearance. And then, there was his father, a retired army officer who had traded in his uniform for farming equipment. The whole family sounded like they could take on the world—or at least win in a game of tug-of-war.

As for me, well, my family story was a lot simpler. It was just my dad and me. I didn't have much to add to Hriday's tale of a bustling household, so I just smiled and nodded, still trying to wrap my head around the fact that I had a six- foot-tall NEET aspirant for a neighbor.

And so, our introduction ended on that note—Hriday with his big family and even bigger presence, and me with my newfound determination to make sure I kept up with this unexpected giant next door.

My classes were set to begin on Monday, and since my institute was conveniently located right next to Hriday's, we decided it made perfect sense to attend them together. Having a buddy to walk with seemed like a good idea— plus, it would be reassuring to have a familiar face around in a new place. So, we agreed to kick off the new week by heading to our respective classes side by side, like two soldiers marching off to battle (well, one soldier and one slightly nervous recruit).

After Hriday left my room, I picked up my pen, ready to dive back into organizing my routine. I was determined to map out my study schedule and get everything in order before the week started. But just as I was about to put pen to paper, there was another knock on the door.

I looked up, a bit surprised by the interruption. "Who is it?" I called out, half-expecting some sort of déjà vu.

And sure enough, the response came back exactly the same as before: "It's me."

I couldn't help but laugh to myself. It seemed Hriday had either forgotten something or decided to drop by again for another reason—or maybe he just wanted to double-check that I hadn't run off in terror after our initial meeting. Either way, I was starting to think that "It's me" was going to become the catchphrase of the day.

When I opened the door, the familiar sight greeted me once again. "Hey, there's a fair by the pond next door. Want to check it out?" he asked with a grin.

"A fair? In Kota? What kind of fair is it?" I asked.

"Suicide," he replied casually. "It's a regular event around here. Prelims results came out yesterday. Someone probably didn't make the cut and took a dip in the pond—permanently."

I was stunned by what he said—"Suicide Fair?" Until now, I had only heard in the news about the frequent suicides in Kota, with students driven to despair by the pressure of exams and the overwhelming stress when they couldn't clear them.

But nothing could have prepared me for the scene at the pond. There, thousands of young people were packed into the fair as if it were the hottest event in town. And the most shocking part? It was all organized by one of their own!

"The person who had my room before me took his own life in the exact same way," Hriday said to me.

"The person who had my current room cleared the prelims and went to Delhi for mains preparation," I replied.

"You're lucky," Hriday remarked.

When I saw the body, it appeared to be a man of about 25 or 26 years old. He was dressed in a blue checkered shirt and black trousers. A raksha sutra, a protective thread, was wrapped around his wrist, and a black thread was tied around his leg. A red necklace hung around his neck, adding to the traditional symbols. We all stood just outside the police barricades, observing the scene in somber silence.

I asked Hriday, "If you don't get selected, will you also end up drowning in the pond?" His eyes met mine with resolve as he replied, "Never." Those words echoed with such certainty, yet now, standing over the lifeless body before me, I couldn't help but reflect on the tragic irony. How much different this outcome might have been if that young man had possessed even a fraction of Hriday's resilience. Perhaps, if he had shared that same determination, he too might have found a way to rise above despair, instead of succumbing to the depths.

Stephen Hawking once said, "However difficult life may seem, there's always something you can do and succeed at." I wish this young man had seen that quote; maybe it would've given him a bit of hope or a different way of looking at his problems.

I muttered to myself, "Well, I've read it, and I know that I'd never end up in the pond, whether I pass my JEE or not. That's just not my style, you won't find me taking a swan dive into the nearest pond. I'm more likely to drown my sorrows in pizza and Netflix."

"Want some tea?" Hriday asked, as if it was the most normal question in the world.

"Now!?... Here?" I replied, my eyebrows shooting up in disbelief.

"Yes, absolutely," Hriday said with a grin, pointing to the north. About 100 meters away, a boy of around 12 or 13 was energetically yelling, *"Chai, chai, garam chai,"* while juggling a kettle and a stack of paper cups. *It was as if the universe had decided that no matter where you are, there's always time for tea.*

And nearly everyone in the crowd was sipping tea. I thought, "Who could resist? I might as well join them."

Sometimes, I wonder if the 12-year-old tea seller's life is, in some ways, better than that of the 25-year-old who didn't make it. At least the boy is still alive, carrying on with his day, one cup of tea at a time.

Just as I wrapped my fingers around the warm cup of tea, feeling the comfort of that first sip, a siren blared through the air, breaking the moment. It was the unmistakable sound of an approaching minister. I looked up and saw a convoy of sleek black SUVs slicing through the crowd like a hot knife through butter.

The vehicles came to a sudden stop, and before I could even process what was happening, a small army of uniformed guards sprang out, moving with military precision. They began clearing a path with the efficiency of someone shooing pigeons from a park bench. The crowd, once a sea of relaxed tea drinkers, suddenly parted like the Red Sea, their curiosity and restlessness rising in waves.

I couldn't help but laugh, thinking, "Well, this is a twist. Here I am, just trying to enjoy my tea, and suddenly I'm part of a live-action political drama! Who knew chai came with a VIP show?"

As the minister stepped out of the first SUV, they wore a face of sympathy so polished it could have been used for a high-end commercial. Dressed in a spotless white kurta with a tricolor scarf draped just so, they moved like a model on a runway—except the runway was a chaotic street, and the audience was eagerly sipping tea.

Their shoes, glistening under the sun, seemed determined to outshine the spotlight they were under. The convoy was surrounded by a parade of supporters and local party members, each adding their own touch to the extravagant display. The crowd, initially focused on their tea, now shifted their curiosity to the minister's grand entrance.

All cameras were trained on the minister, and reporters buzzed with anticipation. It was as if a thousand microphones had suddenly sprouted, each one thrust forward in a competitive frenzy to catch the minister's every word. The air crackled with excitement as everyone held their breath, waiting for the first utterance of the day.

The minister cleared their throat and began, "I am deeply saddened to learn that we have lost a young life among us." Their tone dripped with sympathy, as if they were reading from a script meant to evoke maximum emotion. They then promised to meet with the boy's family and offer as much assistance as possible.

A boy beside me and Hriday whispered, "I've seen seven suicides in Kota before, but this is the first time a minister has shown up.

"There's an election next month," the little tea seller *remarked*, with a hint of knowing as he served another cup.

The minister, glancing at the police inspector, issued a stern directive: "Find out where this boy is from and what his name is—quickly."

The police inspector sprang into action, heading straight to the scene. He barked orders at a constable, who immediately began scouring the area for information. After a diligent search, the constable approached, holding up an ID card he had discovered.

"Sir, there's an ID card around the boy's neck!" the constable announced, his voice carrying a mix of urgency and relief.

"What's his name?" the police inspector asked, leaning in for the answer.

"Abhishek Singh!!" the constable replied, holding up the card as if it were a prize.

CHAPTER FIVE

THAT BROWN HAIR

My first day in Kota was the scariest day of my life. When I lay down on the bed, I couldn't sleep. Creating a routine was out of the question; I couldn't even bring myself to pick up a pen. I was terrified because I was in the same room where the previous occupant had committed suicide earlier that day. The walls were covered with Abhishek Singh's hard work, reminders of his struggles and efforts.

Somehow, morning came. I hadn't planned anything, and today was the first day of coaching class. I managed to convince myself to focus on the upcoming class. As I walked into the class, I remembered reading in a book that if you have a clear why, you can bear almost anyhow.

When I stepped into the classroom, the walls were painted a dull beige, adorned with posters of scientific formulas and motivational quotes. Large windows on one side offered a view of the bustling street outside. At the front, a whiteboard and a teacher's desk cluttered with papers and textbooks set the stage for intense learning. I saw around 150-200 students. I had topped my school, so I was confident that not everyone here could be toppers. My confidence peaked when the physics teacher started teaching calculus, which I had already studied. I eagerly waited for the teacher to ask a question so I could answer, but unfortunately, it was the first day, so they didn't ask any questions.

The chemistry class was boring. Honestly, I find chemistry itself boring. If it were up to me, I'd remove it from the syllabus. In the physics class, I wanted the teacher to ask questions, but the opposite happened. The chemistry teacher did ask a question, and although I knew the answer, I lacked the confidence to respond. This place wasn't like my school where if I didn't react, nobody else would either. A girl sitting three seats ahead in the corner raised her hand. Her brown hair looked like a waterfall flowing down her shoulders.

"Sir, it's 3-ethyl pentane-2-ol," she said.

"Brilliant! Clap for this girl," the teacher said.

The class applauded, and I couldn't help but feel a mix of admiration and envy. Later, in the cafeteria, I spotted her sitting alone at a table, scribbling away in her notebook. The cafeteria was buzzing with activity: students chatted loudly, trays clattered, and the smell of food filled the air. Gathering my courage, I walked up to her.

"Hi," I said nervously. She looked up. "Hello."

"That was impressive in chemistry class," I said, trying to sound casual.

"Thanks! I just love chemistry," she replied, her eyes lighting up.

"I can't stand it," I admitted with a laugh.

"Well, everyone has their preferences," she said with a shrug. "What's your favorite subject?"

"Physics," I said.

"Really? I'm struggling with calculus," she confessed. "Maybe we can help each other out?" I suggested. "That sounds like a plan," she said with a smile.

Her name was Ananya and she was from Jaipur. One day, during one of our many conversations, she told me about the beautiful palaces and forts there.

"I'd love to visit Jaipur someday," I said. "You're welcome to come anytime," she replied.

"My parents wanted me to get into a good engineering college," she said. "It's a lot of pressure, but they're very supportive. And you?"

"Ahh... I want to do something with Physics. Mechanics is my favorite. I want to do Electrical Engineering."

"I want to become a writer. Ananya told me. But, with my preparation for JEE, I hardly have any time to write properly. I want to become the best writer in India."

"Why not the best in the world?" I asked.

"That's hard!" she exclaimed, her eyes widening and her mouth dropping open in surprise, to the point where her brown curls nearly covered her eyes.

"JEE is hard too," I said with a smile.

"Indeed, it is. That's why I'm so frustrated!" she said.

"Why don't you tell your parents that you want to be a writer?" I asked.

"I did," she replied, "but they believe I can do that after JEE."

"Well, they're not wrong. What's the problem with that?"

"The problem is that JEE is hard, sir!" she said, gathering her notebooks before flashing a quick smile. "Goodbye!" she added, turning and walking away, her brown hair cascading like a waterfall behind her.

Moments after she left, a boy slid into the seat where Ananya had just been. His face was clouded with sadness. I recognized him from class—he was in my batch.

"Vishal, right? Did you solve the physics problems that Sir gave us yesterday?" I asked him.

"No," he replied.

After 2-3 minutes of silence, he said, "What the hell are we all doing? Tell me, do you think everyone who comes here will crack the exam? There's so much competition."

"Yeah, there is competition, but that's what we're made for. If we don't participate in competition, how will we realize our potential?" I said.

"Your philosophy is good, but isn't it destroying the country? Students who could contribute in better ways are getting trapped here," Vishal argued.

"In what better way? I don't think there's any other way to help the country except through studying. Study is the ultimate thing that develops a person intellectually and from every perspective," I said.

"I don't think calculus will ever help me in my life!" Vishal debated.

"That depends on how you approach it. My dad used to say that **great learners always have the art of receptivity**. If you want to learn, try to grasp things as they are. If you study physics, study like a physicist. If you study math, study like a mathematician. Well, I personally don't know about chemistry. It all works if you like studying. If you find it difficult to develop an interest in studying, leave it and find your passion. Because until your 'why' is not clear, you'll struggle to find the 'how.'

"The system doesn't give us the independence to find our 'why.' We're all trapped," Vishal said, frustrated.

"I don't know what's wrong or right, but for me, achieving the priorities I set for myself matters more than anything else," I said simply.

"Well, my priority now is to leave this institute, which I'm going to do. I'm going back home, and I'm sure one day I'll hire all you engineers," Vishal mentioned with attitude.

"Ah, that's great. All the best," I said to him.

The first mock test was coming up, and I was deep into revising my chemistry notes which had been given by Ananya, when I heard a knock on the door.

"Who's there?" I asked without looking up. "It's me," came the familiar voice.

I knew exactly who it was. "Of course, Hriday."

When I opened the door, Hriday's smiling face greeted me. "Chai peene chalega?" he asked with a cheerful grin.

I sighed and looked at my notes. "The test is tomorrow." Hriday wasn't giving up. "We'll be back in five minutes." I shook my head. "Not now, please."

Hriday leaned on the doorframe, a playful look in his eyes.

"If it were that girl with the brown hair, you'd be out the door already."

I gave him a look. "The test is more important, bro."

Hriday laughed and shrugged, knowing he wouldn't change my mind.

The clock ticked past midnight, and I finally allowed myself a few hours of sleep.

The next morning, I woke up early, revised the syllabus, and headed to class. As I entered, I immediately noticed Ananya. She looked tense—her face pale, eyes hollow, and her hands fidgeting restlessly. Something was off. I walked over to her, concerned, and asked about her preparation.

"I'm not prepared at all," she muttered, her voice trembling with a mix of anxiety and exhaustion. Her eyes darted around the room like she was trapped. "I feel so stressed, I can't take this anymore. I... I just want it all to stop," she whispered, her voice breaking. "Yesterday, I got an offer from a magazine company for some blogs I submitted, and for a moment, it felt like an escape. But I'd have to move to Bangalore for the job. I told my father, and of course, he didn't agree. He wants me to stay here and crack the exam —just like everyone else does."

Her hands tightened into fists as she spoke. "I haven't studied for today's test. Not a single page. I can't even think straight. What's the point?" Her voice dropped to a barely audible whisper. "I'm done pretending like I can handle this... maybe I don't even want to."

She stared blankly ahead for a moment, as if lost in a place I couldn't reach, then abruptly stood up, shaking her head. "I'll probably just scrape by in chemistry," she added, though her tone was hollow and distant. Without waiting for a reply, she moved to her seat, leaving me with a sinking feeling in my chest. Something was seriously wrong.

I was just thinking about how I could help her when the mock test paper appeared in front of me. At that moment, I decided that concentrating on the test was more important. While taking the test, I didn't even realize that Ananya had finished her paper and left. After my test was over, I went to the cafeteria where she usually stayed, but I couldn't find her there.

I immediately called Hriday and explained the entire situation to him. He listened intently and then said, "This is really concerning. We need to find her right away. Stay at the cafeteria; I'll be there soon."

Hriday arrived shortly and asked, "Did you call Ananya?" "She's not answering."

"She might have gone back to her hostel," Hriday suggested. We decided to check there and headed towards her hostel.

But before we could enter the hostel, we saw a guard standing right at the gate. The area was brightly lit by the midday sun, casting sharp shadows on the ground. The hostel building stood tall, its windows reflecting the sunlight.

The guard was tall and strong, with a thick mustache and a serious look on his face. He wore a dark blue uniform, making him look even more imposing. His eyes were fixed on us, narrowing as we got closer. He stood very still, glaring at us as if he was ready to stop us from going any further.

"Hey, you fools, where do you think you're going?" the guard snapped, clearly annoyed. "Can't you see the sign? This is a girls' hostel!" He stared at us with a look of anger.

"Please, let us in," I pleaded with the guard, sounding desperate. Despite our efforts, he wouldn't let us enter. I felt lost, not knowing what to do next.

Just then, a dark blue car pulled up at the hostel gate, catching our attention. The man who stepped out of the car looked important. He walked up to the guard and said firmly, "I am Ananya's father." The guard's face immediately showed respect.

We quickly moved forward and spoke to Ananya's father. "Sir, we are Ananya's friends," I said urgently. "She was very stressed during the exam today, and she's not answering my calls. We're really worried about her."

The guard, now focused on Ananya's father, seemed to rethink his decision. We stood there, the tension still thick in the air, waiting for what would happen next.

Finally, her father agreed to let us come along. We followed him to Ananya's hostel room, hoping to find her and offer some support. When we arrived, we noticed that the door was locked, which suggested that she hadn't returned to her room.

I turned to Ananya's father and explained, "She was extremely stressed out today, and she hasn't been answering my calls." He listened carefully, and then he told us that he had received a message from her earlier in the morning. The message simply read, "Papa, I can't." That was all it said, and it left us both deeply worried.

"I tried calling her several times after receiving that message," he continued, "but she didn't pick up any of my calls." His face grew even more anxious as he realized the gravity of the situation. We stood there, unsure of what to do next, with the locked door and our growing fear making the moment even more tense.

Since Ananya's mother had arrived, she hadn't stopped crying. Hriday tried to console her, but she wouldn't calm down. Ananya's mother turned to her husband and tearfully asked, "What was the need to send her here?"

Ananya's father reacted casually to this, saying, "I know my daughter. She would never do something like what you're thinking."

We were at a loss, not knowing what to do next. The air was thick with worry and confusion. Ananya's mother, still crying uncontrollably, couldn't be consoled. Ananya's father, though trying to stay calm, looked deeply worried. Finally, Hriday, with a determined look in his eyes, suggested, "We should report this to the police."

As we were about to leave for the police station, my eyes went to the gate. There was Ananya, her brown hair falling like a waterfall on her shoulders as she walked towards us, adjusting it.

Relief washed over us as we saw her. "Ananya!" I called out, my voice trembling with a mix of fear and hope.

Ananya looked up, startled to see us all there. She hurried towards us, concern evident on her face. "What are you all doing here?" she asked, glancing at her parents.

Her mother rushed to her, tears streaming down her face. "Where were you? We were so worried!" she cried, hugging Ananya tightly.

Ananya's father, though visibly relieved, tried to maintain his composure. "You didn't answer your phone," he said, his voice stern but gentle.

"Sorry, Papa, I had put my phone on flight mode, so I didn't see the calls. And even now, it's still on flight mode," Ananya explained.

"But where were you?" I asked.

"I went to a yoga ashram for meditation, I was feeling anxious," Ananya explained. "I had mentioned it to you this morning."

"I was sure my daughter wouldn't do something like this.

She's strong. But what about that message? 'Papa, I can't'?" Ananya's father asked her.

"I sent that message about the JEE, Papa. I was feeling overwhelmed and didn't want to stay here. My tests haven't gone well either," Ananya explained.

"You're not going to stay here anymore," Ananya's mother said firmly. "We are here to take you home."

Ananya looked at her father to gauge his reaction. After a moment, he agreed but added, "We're not sending you to Bangalore. You can do your work from home."

"We'll take care of it later," Ananya's mother said.

"I don't think you need to learn calculus anymore," I said with a forced smile.

"I can still learn it, if Papa says so," Ananya replied.

"No, there's no need for that. You're coming with us," Ananya's father said.

Finally, Ananya was leaving to prioritize her goals. I was happy for her, but also sad, knowing I wouldn't see her brown hair anymore.

We helped her pack her things, and just as she was about to leave, I asked her, "If your father hadn't come here, what would you have done?"

She smiled and replied, "I'd be doing what I was doing— studying calculus. I might get depressed, but I never give up."

Hearing this, I muttered, "Ved is too just like that." "Ved?" she asked, a little surprised.

"Ah, never mind. All the best for your next journey," I said excitedly.

"Thanks," she replied. "By the way, I have something for you. Just a minute."

"Is she going to give you her chemistry notes?" Hriday muttered.

"Who knows?" I replied, feeling overwhelmed.

Ananya brought a book from her bag and handed it to me with deep affection and seriousness. "I hope you get something good out of it. Have a good read," she said, and then turned away, getting into her dark blue car. That was the last time I saw her brown hair.

"What's the book?" Hriday asked.

"Ah, it's The Bird of Time by Sarojini Naidu," I replied.

CHAPTER SIX

INNER WIN : Priorities Matters

I stood in the middle of the chaos, a tornado of textbooks and emotions swirling around me. The emptiness Ananya's departure left in my life was like a missing sock in the laundry—impossible to ignore and oddly irritating. My studies were the only thing holding me together. One day, while going over my chemistry notes, which had started to carry the faint scent of Ananya's brown curls from flipping through them so much, my phone rang.

Usually, it was Dad calling, checking in like he always did. But given the time, I figured he was busy. My heart skipped a beat—could it be Ananya? I rushed to the window where my phone was, only to see Ved's name on the screen.

I can't lie—I was ridiculously happy, like a kid finding an extra fry at the bottom of the bag. Ved was calling! After six long months in Kota, this was the first time he'd dialed me up. I answered so fast I nearly dropped the phone.

"How are you, man?" Ved's voice came through. I paused, unsure of what to say. I had been okay, but now? Now, I felt like I'd just found a lifeline. That call from Ved was the best thing that had happened all week, and I was happy to hear his familiar voice after all this time.

"I'm good," I managed to say. "How about you?" I asked Vedant.

"I'm the best, as always," Ved replied with his usual confidence. "Just wrapped up a match."

"Oh, there was a match today? How did it go?" I asked, genuinely curious.

"We batted first. I scored 110 runs, and we put up 272 on the board. Took 2 catches, made a stumping, and we won by 65 runs," he said, sounding as proud as ever.

"How's your prep going?" he asked, shifting gears.

"Pretty well! I actually got full marks on my last test," I said, maybe showing off just a little.

"Doremon sir was asking about you today," he added, referring to our old school teacher who we used to call Doremon because he looked so much like the cartoon character.

"Oh yeah? What did he say?" I asked, curious.

"He was joking that he could've taught you better physics than what you're learning in Kota," Ved said with a laugh.

"Haha, I miss him. Tell him I said namaste," I replied, grinning at the thought.

"How's Dadi?" I asked, wanting to check in.

"She's busy with her usual worship," Ved answered, sounding fond.

Talking to Ved was just what I needed. It lifted my spirits and gave me a boost of motivation. Just as I hung up, feeling lighter, there was a knock at the door.

"Who's there?" I called out. No answer.

The knock came again, a bit more insistent this time. "Who's there?" I asked once more, a little louder.

I paused, thinking that if it were Hriday, he would've said, "It's me" by now. Who could it be? "Hriday?" I asked, my voice tinged with uncertainty.

"Yes," came the reply, but it was soft—softer than Hriday's usual cheerful tone.

Curious, I decided to open the door, and there he was— Hriday, standing in the dim light of the hallway.

"You didn't say anything, so I was wondering who it could be," I said, managing a small smile. But as I looked closer, I noticed the tears welling up in his eyes. My smile faded.

"What's wrong? Why are you crying?" I asked, feeling a sudden pang of worry.

In a voice that trembled with urgency, he said, "I'm going home. I don't know if I'll be back. You can take my notes; they might help you." He hesitated for a moment, and then, almost as if the words were too heavy to bear, he added, "My father is no more. I'm leaving."

Before I could react, he handed me his room keys, his movements quick and almost desperate. Then, without another word, he turned and walked away, leaving me standing there, rooted in shock, a deep sadness settling over me like the evening mist.

I stood there for a long moment, the weight of Hriday's words pressing down on me. The keys felt cold in my hand, but my mind was numb, struggling to process what had just happened. The hallway seemed darker now, the silence deeper. I wanted to say something, anything, but the words wouldn't come.

As Hriday's footsteps faded away, I finally closed the door, leaning against it as a heavy sigh escaped me. The room felt emptier than before, the walls closing in with a quiet stillness that made the loneliness even more profound. I glanced at the pile of notes Hriday had left behind, now imbued with a sense of loss that hadn't been there before.

Sleep was elusive that night. I tossed and turned, my thoughts a tangled mess of memories and worry for Hriday. The darkness outside matched the one I felt inside, each passing hour marked by the faint chime of the wall clock. Eventually, exhaustion took over, and I drifted off, but even my dreams were heavy with sorrow.

The next morning, I couldn't focus in class at all. My mind kept drifting back to Hriday's situation. He was on the verge of taking his medical entrance exams, and now everything had come crashing down. What would he do if he didn't come back? The thought haunted me, making it hard to think about anything else.

Lost in these thoughts, I barely noticed the world around me until I suddenly heard a voice. It was faint at first, almost like it was coming from far away, but then it grew sharper. I snapped back to reality and realized someone was calling my name. When I looked around, I saw the entire class staring at me, and at the front, the chemistry teacher was glaring, his eyes narrowing with a mixture of irritation and concern.

"Are you asleep?" the teacher's voice cut through the room sharply. "Go and wash your face!"

The class burst into laughter, but my cheeks flushed with embarrassment. I made my way to the washroom, each step heavy with the weight of my mortification.

As I neared the washroom, a piercing scream shattered the air—a long, agonizing wail that seemed to reverberate through the very walls. The sound was so raw and distressing that it froze me in place. Every instinct screamed at me to turn back, but I stood paralyzed, staring at the washroom door.

The scream continued, its intensity rising and falling in a rhythm of pure terror. The commotion quickly drew attention; within moments, the institute's peon appeared, his face a mask of urgent concern. He rushed towards the source of the noise, his steps quick and determined.

"What happened?" he asked, his voice urgent and sharp.

"I—I don't know," I replied, my voice trembling. "I just came to wash my face."

Without waiting for further explanations, the peon entered the washroom, leaving me to stand outside, my heart pounding with anxiety. The atmosphere grew increasingly tense as more teachers arrived, their faces etched with worry. The corridor filled with a murmur of hushed voices and concerned glances.

Soon, a small crowd of teachers gathered around the washroom door, their expressions grave as they attempted to piece together the situation. The commotion continued, but their focus remained on understanding the source of the harrowing scream.

As a student, I was quickly moved away from the scene, the seriousness of the situation becoming increasingly apparent. I returned to my classroom, feeling the weight of the incident like a physical presence. When I sat down, a heavy silence had fallen over the school. The usual chatter was replaced by an uneasy quiet, and within minutes, classes were dismissed abruptly.

The entire atmosphere was tinged with a sense of foreboding, a shared unease that something profoundly unsettling had occurred within the confines of that washroom.

Everyone was sent back to the hostel. When I returned, I was overwhelmed with questions from fellow students, each inquiry adding to my mounting confusion. The evening passed in a blur, and the door remained silent— Hriday was gone. I found myself pondering whom I could even share a cup of tea with. I thought about calling Dad for comfort but decided to turn to the book Ananya had given me instead.

Just as I settled down to read, my phone buzzed with a notification.

"Classes are suspended for the next few days due to a tragic accident at the institute."

A tragic accident? The words echoed in my mind as I struggled to connect them with the earlier events. The realization sent a cold shiver down my spine. Was this related to the horrifying scream from the washroom?

I quickly checked the news on my phone, and the horrifying truth emerged. A boy had hanged himself in the institute's washroom and died. The details were grim. The boy had wanted to withdraw from his preparation and return home but was met with refusal when he asked for a refund for the remaining year of his tuition, despite having paid for it in full. His family was facing severe financial difficulties, and the money was urgently needed. Unable to find another way out, he had taken this tragic and desperate step.

My shock deepened as I read the boy's name: Vishal. Just a few days ago, I had spoken with Vishal. He had mentioned his plans to leave the institute. The realization that someone I had interacted with had met such a tragic end left me reeling.

I was overwhelmed with stress, feeling crushed by everything happening around me. Abhishek Singh's tragedy still haunted me, and Ananya's departure left a void. Hriday leaving only added to the emptiness. Now, this heartbreaking incident with Vishal felt like the final straw, driving home how hard life is for young people in our country. It all felt like too much to handle.

At that point, I realized I had only one choice: to go back home. The institute was shutting down temporarily, and with no classes running, there was no reason to stay. This situation only deepened my belief that decision-making for young people in our nation is incredibly tough, often leading to heartbreak and loss. The weight of these challenges felt unbearable.

#Solitude

The next few days were a blur of overwhelming emotions. The tragedies seemed to pile up one after another— Abhishek Singh's untimely demise, Ananya's departure, Hriday leaving without a proper goodbye, and now, Vishal's tragic end. I felt like I was drowning in a sea of grief and confusion, each event pulling me further into the depths of despair. I was left alone with my thoughts, which were anything but comforting.

I couldn't concentrate on my studies; my mind was constantly wrestling with itself. On one side was the voice that urged me to leave, to escape the pain and uncertainty. It whispered that going home was the only way to find peace. On the other side was a quieter, more stubborn voice that refused to back down. This voice reminded me that running away wouldn't solve anything, that *the real battle I needed to fight was within myself. It was me versus me, and there was no easy way out.*

One evening, as I sat in my dimly lit room, I reached for the book Ananya had given me, The Bird of Time by Sarojini Naidu. I had looked it few times, but something compelled me to read it now. As I flipped through the pages, I found lines that spoke directly to my situation:

"The bird of time has but a little way to fly—and lo, the bird is on the wing."

These words resonated deeply, reminding me of the urgency of making the most of the time I had. I realized then that this was my moment of decision. I could either let the tragedies around me define my path, or I could choose to fight—fight against the part of me that wanted to give up, fight to stay, and fight to find my own strength.

With a deep breath, I made my choice. I would stay. I would confront the fear and uncertainty head-on. This was a battle I needed to fight, not against the world, but against my own inner demons.

The days that followed were not easy. The memories of Ananya, Hriday and Vishal's death, the haunting silence of the hostel, and the constant temptation to give up were always there, lurking in the back of my mind. But each time the urge to run away surfaced, I reminded myself of the resolve I had found in Sarojini Naidu's words. I pushed through the pain, focusing on my studies with a renewed sense of purpose.

The fear and doubt that had once held me back started to lose their grip. I was growing stronger, more resilient, and more confident with each passing day in solitude.

Then, after a few weeks, the institute reopened. But those weeks had been among the most transformative of my life. In that time of solitude, I had come to understand my inner thoughts and priorities more clearly. I realized that amidst all the chaos and loss, my true priority was to succeed in the JEE exams, which I set myself. I had believed in myself and my ability to achieve it, despite the odds.

The absence of distractions allowed me to delve deeper into my thoughts, to understand the true nature of the battle I was fighting. It wasn't about the external events that had shaken me; it was about overcoming the obstacles within myself.

As the weeks passed, I realized that the greatest battles are the ones we fight with ourselves. They are the most challenging, but they also lead to the most profound growth. I had faced my fears, confronted my doubts, and emerged stronger on the other side.

The experience left me with a deep sense of accomplishment and a new understanding of resilience. I had learned that true strength comes from within, and that no matter how difficult the journey, it's the fight against our own inner struggles that defines who we are. The tragedies that had once seemed overwhelming were now part of my story—chapters in a book that I was still writing, with many more pages yet to be filled.

And so, I continued on, not just as a student preparing for exams, but as someone who had fought and won the most important battle of all—the battle with myself.

HARD SLAP

Kota felt like a boot camp, but instead of a tough instructor shouting orders, I had textbooks and a study schedule that didn't know what weekends were. For two years, I had been wrestling with trigonometry, chemistry formulas, and the dreaded mock tests. If there was a prize for surviving on chai, I would have won it easily.

The past months felt like I was on a tough reality show where the challenges included solving a hundred math problems before breakfast and cramming all of physics into my brain by midnight. There were days when I was sure the only thing I'd master was how to make the perfect cup of tea. Probably.

But now, with my bags packed and my study notes stuffed into every corner of my suitcase, I was ready to leave Kota behind. I looked at my room one last time—the place where I had daily battles with equations that just wouldn't listen, and where I'd told myself every single day that I'd quit and become a monk if I saw another integration problem. Yet, somehow, I'd made it through.

Dragging my overstuffed suitcase towards the station, I couldn't help but laugh at how silly it all seemed. Who knew the hardest part of Kota would be fitting two years' worth of study material into one bag? It felt like trying to solve a puzzle that had no solution.

As I boarded the train, I felt a strange mix of tiredness and excitement. I'd survived Kota. If that wasn't a reason to smile, I didn't know what was. I mentally patted myself on the back, but then remembered the real challenge was still ahead—my 12th board exams and the JEE, back in Lucknow.

As the train chugged along, I started feeling a bit emotional. Going back to Gomtinagar, Lucknow, felt like returning to a time when life was simpler, when stress meant deciding which movie to watch on a Sunday. Now, I was coming back with the battle scars of two years in Kota and a new appreciation for sleep.

I imagined meeting Ved again—my best friend who hadn't faced the Kota grind. While I was busy wrestling with textbooks, he had been living the good life, or so I thought. Would he see the guy who had stared down organic chemistry and somehow made it through, even if it meant losing some sleep and gaining a few gray hairs?

When the train finally chugged into Lucknow, I couldn't help but grin. It felt like I was returning as a hero—though my battles were with question papers, not dragons. The familiar smell of the city hit me as soon as I stepped off the train, and I knew I was home.

But before facing the board exams and JEE, I had a more urgent mission: catching up with Ved. And with Ved, even a simple catch-up could turn into an adventure worthy of a sitcom. Tomorrow is Sunday, so there will surely be a jalebi party at his place. I'll make sure to get there with jalebis before seven, I thought as I drifted off to sleep that night.

Sunday mornings in Gomti Nagar were always sweet and delightful, thanks to Ramu Bhaiya's famous jalebis. After two yers away, I was finally witnessing another morning in Gomti Nagar... everything was just the same: the warm, slightly polluted air, the barking dogs, and the old lady with a broom in her hand, who swept the streets every morning. Soon, those streets would be littered with the discarded leaf plates of the *jalebi* lovers who flocked to Ramu Bhaiya's shop.

I parked my red *Flame Kaiser*—my trusty bicycle, inspired by a cartoon—right in front of the Shiva temple. As I walked towards Ramu Bhaiya's stall, the enticing aroma of hot, freshly fried jalebis soaking in sugary syrup filled the air, making my mouth water.

I couldn't help but smile at the thought of surprising Ved with these jalebis after two whole years. I imagined Dadi's warm smile, Rima Aunty's delight, and Mr. Sharma's reaction—though I wasn't sure if he'd be happier to see me or the jalebis. The thought added to my excitement.

"Quickly pack some jalebis and dahi, Ramu Bhaiya!" I hurriedly requested. It had been two years since I last visited his shop, but he still served me first. As I waited, he asked me to tutor his son, Suraj, who was preparing for his tenth-grade exams. But I politely declined, reminding him that I had my own battle ahead with the JEE.

When I finally arrived at Ved's house with the jalebis and dahi hanging from my bicycle, the old buzz and excitement came rushing back. The aroma of Rima Aunty's parathas wafted from the kitchen window to where I stood at the door. Mr. Sharma was probably still asleep, Dadi must be busy with her puja preparations, and Radhika Didi might have gone to the library. But where was Ved? I chuckled at the thought—probably getting ready to go out for jalebis himself!

Sure enough, there he was, stepping outside and twirling his scooty keys like Lord Vishnu's Sudarshan Chakra. He was still the same, just a bit taller, and oh boy, his beard had really filled out... The moment he spotted me on the balcony, his face lit up with surprise and joy. "No way, is that you?" he exclaimed, clearly amazed to see me after two years. His reaction was so genuine, it felt like we had picked up right where we left off. He welcomed me with open arms and a grin that made me feel instantly at home.

"When did you get here?" he asked. "Just last night," I replied.

As soon as we sat down at the dining table, which was accessible from the balcony, Dadi walked in with her usual basket full of flowers and a glass of milk in hand. I quickly stood up and bent down to touch her feet.

"Bhole Baba bless you," she said with a warm smile, her voice carrying the distinct Varanasi accent that reminded me of her roots in Kashi.

Just then, Mr. Sharma waddled out of the bedroom into the hall, his belly looking even more rounded, like a well- risen dough. His cheeks had plumped up too, probably thanks to Rima Aunty's relentless paratha campaign. And just as I was thinking about those parathas, in walked Rima Aunty, but instead of her usual golden-brown parathas, she was holding a plate of... white discs? Wait, were those idlis? Yep, she had traded in the parathas for a South Indian twist today.

South Indian breakfast paired with jalebi? Wow! Honestly, it was a "Perfectly made in heaven" breakfast.

As soon as Mr. Sharma's eyes landed on the jalebis, he asked, with the urgency of a man on a mission, "Dahi!?"

"Oh yes, Uncle, I brought some!" I quickly pulled out the dahi, remembering how he always insisted that dahi with jalebi was practically a healthy food.

He looked at me with such affection in his eyes, like I'd just passed some kind of test by remembering his favorite combo.

Just then, Radhika didi stormed into the hall, I could tell something was seriously wrong. Her usually calm face was now flushed with anger, and the way she tossed her bag onto the sofa placed in the balcony made the hall fall silent. Even Ved, who was halfway through a joke, stopped mid- sentence. I had never seen Radhika didi like this before, and trust me, I've seen her scold Ved plenty of times.

"What happened, didi?" Ved asked.

Radhika didi didn't answer right away. She was pacing towards us, her hands clenched into fists, her eyes filled with a fury that could only mean one thing—trouble. "That Vikki Chaturvedi," she finally spat out, her voice trembling with disgust. "He thinks he can scare me? Just because he's Seenu Chaturvedi's brother, he thinks he can get away with anything!"

I exchanged a worried glance with Ved. Vikki Chaturvedi was notorious in Gomti Nagar. He was the kind of guy who thrived on power, using his brother's position as an MLA to bully anyone who crossed his path. Everyone knew about him, but no one dared to confront him—except Radhika didi, apparently.

But this wasn't just about some petty fight. Vikki had a reputation for being dangerous. He had been harassing people for years, including Amir's family. I still remember how devastated Amir was after his sister, Fatima, took her own life. She had been a bright, spirited girl, but Vikki's relentless threats had broken her. And then there was Mr. Siddiqui, Amir's father, who had been struggling ever since, haunted by the loss of his daughter and the fact that Vikki walked free.

"He dared to approach me today," she continued, her voice growing steadier as she spoke. "He tried to pull the same nonsense with me that he's pulled with Fatima and so many others. But I wasn't going to let him get away with it. I told him exactly what I thought of him—and his so-called power."

Ved and I were stunned. Radhika didi was brave, no doubt about that, but Vikki wasn't just some neighborhood thug. He was dangerous, and his brother's influence made him nearly untouchable.

"What did you say to him?" I asked, my curiosity piqued but also a little worried for her.

She suddenly noticed me, her stern expression softening just a bit. "Ohhh! When did you come back from Kota?"

"Never mind," I said, eager to get back to the story. "What did you say to him?"

"I told him that his threats mean nothing to me," she said, her eyes blazing with determination. "I told him that if he ever tried to mess with me or anyone I care about again, I would make sure the whole city knew what a coward he is. He didn't expect that. He's used to people cowering in fear, but today, he met someone who wasn't afraid to fight back."

Mr. Sharma's expression grew serious, and he put down his Jalebi. "Radhika, you know how dangerous that family can be. They have power, and they won't hesitate to use it."

"I know, Papa," she replied, her voice calm but resolute. "But someone has to stand up to them. If we all keep quiet, people like Vikki will continue to ruin lives. I won't just sit by and let them destroy more lives."

Rima Aunty smiled at her daughter, but concern lingered in her eyes. She sat down beside Mr. Sharma, quietly observing the unease in the room. "Well, fearlessness is good," she said, "but sometimes, courage means knowing when to choose your battles carefully."

"I think Vikki needs a taste of my bat," Ved said.

"And you need a taste of my slap," Dr. Sharma snapped, his tone stern. "Your 12th board exams are just around the corner, but all I ever see in your hands is that bat, never a book!"

"I'll handle the exams," Ved said casually.

"I'll see about that on the day of the results," Dr. Sharma shot back.

"So, how's the cricket going, Vedant?" I asked.

"U-19 matches are going on," Ved said. "Semis are tomorrow."

"Bhaiya, you're here!?" a voice suddenly called out from the balcony.

"Amir!" I immediately stood up and went to him. "How are you?" I asked. "You've even grown taller than Ved!"

"When did you arrive?" Amir asked.

"Last night. I was just about to come and see you." "Catch up later, Amir. Come on, let's go," Ved said. "Where to?" I asked.

"Amir has become a pace bowler now. You should see his bowling," Vedant said.

"Seriously?" I said, astonished. "Looking at his body, it definitely looks like he's made it happen."

"That's what I missed in Kota—playing with my two buddies again. It was an amazing day. But just like before, after two hours of perfect batting bliss, Ved said, 'I'm really stressed about the exams. I don't even feel like taking them.'"

"Great." I replied on his nonsense.

"I'm really stressed too," Amir added. "I've got my 10th boards coming up as well."

"What are you planning to take up in 11th grade?" I asked. "And how's Abba?"

"I'm planning to go for Maths," Amir said. "Abbu is doing well, but his slaps still pack a punch."

"Why does your father hit you so much?" Ved asked.

"He takes his anger out on me because he can't vent it on anyone else. He's still fuming about those who say Ammi ran away with someone else," Amir explained.

"Amir, did you know that your mother was Seenu and Vikki's maternal sister?" I said.

"Yes, I know. That's why Vikki keeps bothering me," Amir said. "He blames Abbu for everything, thinking it's all his fault. He even says that Abbu killed Ammi, though I don't believe it. "And that's why he keeps threatening to harm both Abbu and me."

"That Vikki is a real scoundrel! He stole my spot in the U- 16 team and didn't even perform in the matches," Ved said angrily. "And tomorrow, we have a match against his team," Ved added.

"Then it's going to be one hell of a match... haha," I said, laughing. "You know what? You should bring Radhika didi to the match tomorrow. Maybe that'll scare the hell out of him!"

"True that," Amir added. "Didi is dangerous!"

"Good thing she's not here right now, or else she'd be dangerous for us!" Ved added, laughing.

The next day, around 8 AM, Amir and I marched to the stadium to back Vedant, pretending the exams next week didn't exist—because priorities, right? We tried everything to drag Radhika didi along, but she gave us the classic "I have a mock test for prelims" excuse. Honestly, who chooses a test over a brother's match?

After that, we swung by Mr. Sharma's place to get him to watch his son's big game. Ved had once confessed how badly he wanted to impress his father, but Mr. Sharma, in his usual style, waved it off with, "I don't have time to melt away my belly fat under the sun."

Dadi, on the other hand, was more excited than all of us combined. It took some serious convincing to get her to stay home, and we had to seal the deal by promising her a VIP seat at the final.

As we arrived at the ground, the sun was climbing higher, casting long shadows across the field. Both teams were warming up, and the air was filled with anticipation. Vedant's team took to batting first, and it was evident from the start that Vedant was in exceptional form. Every shot he played was precise, sending the ball racing to the boundaries. By the time he reached 110 runs, Amir nudged me with a grin and said, "Looks like Ved bhaiya is making a statement today. He's playing like he's got something to prove." I nodded, "Absolutely. It would have been great if Mr. Sharma were here to see this."

After the frst inning sumed up, Vikki stepped up to bat. "Here comes Mr. Swagger," Amir remarked.

Vikki started off slowly but soon found his rhythm. His shots were crisp, and the runs began accumulating quickly. "Is he using a magic wand or something? Every ball seems to find the boundary," Amir observed, his tone a mix of disbelief and frustration, as Vedant's frustration became apparent.

As Vikki's unbeaten 82 sealed the match for his team, Amir let out a sigh and said, "Well, it was a bad day." I glanced at Vedant, who stood behind the stumps, looking disappointed.

As we approached Vedant, he only muttered, "That jerk got lucky."

Today felt like a replay of two years ago. Vedant had scored a hundred in the semi-final, just like before, yet it seemed unlikely he would make the U-19 team. Despite his stellar performance throughout the tournament, the same old doubts were creeping in. The three of us were confident, though, even if the team didn't make it to the finals. Vedant had been a standout throughout, and we were crossing our fingers for his selection, hoping the selectors would see what we saw.

"Well, the selectors were another story, but what Vedant really wanted was for Mr. Sharma to at least see him play."

"Every time there's an important match, the same thing happens—our team gets knocked out," Vedant said, frustration evident in his voice. "And when I go home and tell Papa that we lost, he just thinks sports are a waste of time. He's been glued to his chair since his college days. How do I explain to him what sports really mean?" He sighed, clearly fed up.

"To be honest, even I'm starting to think sports might be a waste of time," I remarked. "What's even happening here? I don't see any future in this."

"I agree with you, bhaiya," Amir chimed in. "Playing for fun is fine, but doing it professionally? That's a huge risk."

Ved didn't say anything; he seemed lost in his thoughts, maybe confused, maybe a little emotional.

"Well, right now we should focus on what's most important," I said. "The board exams start next week. How's your preparation going, Ved?"

"I don't know," Ved muttered, probably looking a bit depressed.

"Not everything can be healed by others; some battles you have to fight on your own. I think Ved is going through that phase right now, just like I did when I was in Kota." I didn't push Ved to talk any further and instead turned to Amir, asking him about his preparation for the 10th board exams. It made me happy to see that, at least, Amir was focused on his studies.

I got caught up in my own board exams and JEE preparations, and in the hustle, I forgot to ask Ved about the U-19 selection. When I finally did, Ved reluctantly mentioned that he wasn't selected again. His voice was flat, and it was clear he hadn't taken the news well. On top of that, it seemed like he wasn't taking his exams seriously either. His focus was scattered, and his usual enthusiasm was missing. The weight of missed opportunities and academic pressures seemed to be taking a toll on him.

As his best friend, I wasn't sure what the best course of action was. I decided to consult my dad about it. He always gives more thoughtful advice compared to Ved and Amir's father. Probably I'd call myself lucky in genetics.

That evening, I went to see Dad. His room was always a sanctuary of calm, a reflection of his own serene demeanor. The atmosphere is always calm, just like Dad. Or maybe, I should say, Dad stays calm in that peaceful setting. One thing I've always noticed is that he usually has a book in hand. This time, he was engrossed in a book about Swami Vivekananda, as evidenced by the picture of Vivekananda on the cover.

"Dad," I whispered softly.

He turned to me with his usual calm. "Where were you all day?" he asked.

"Uh... I went to watch Ved's match. It was the semifinal, the selection match for the U-19 state team."

"Oh, really? So, who won?" "Ved's team lost."

"Hmm... I see." He paused for a moment, then shifted theconversation. "Your exams start next Monday, right?"

"Yeah," I nodded, "but I'm here to ask you about something else."

"What is it?" Dad asked, setting his book aside.

I hesitated for a moment, gathering my thoughts. "I mean... Ved's been trying so hard. But every time, it's like something goes wrong. It's not just once or twice. It's happened before, and now it's happening again. Should he keep going, or is it time to let go?"

Dad leaned back against the headboard of his bed, his eyes thoughtful. "You know," he began, "life isn't as simple as effort in, result out. There's a tendency to believe that if we work hard enough, success is guaranteed. But reality doesn't always follow that path. You can control your effort, but not the outcome."

I frowned, still feeling conflicted. "But if you keep failing, doesn't it mean maybe you're not meant for it? Shouldn't you take that as a sign to stop?"

Dad smiled gently, a wisdom in his expression that I couldn't quite grasp. *"Failure is often seen as a sign of weakness, of not being good enough. But what we forget is that failure is a part of the process.* Sometimes, it's there to teach us resilience. The question isn't whether you're failing. It's whether you're learning from it. Are you growing? Are you becoming stronger, more determined? Or are you letting failure define you?"

I sat quietly, letting his words sink in. "But Dad, it's exhausting. How long can someone keep going when they never win?"

He nodded. "It's tiring, no doubt. But you have to ask yourself what it is you're truly chasing. Is it just the win? The recognition? Or is it something deeper, something that can't be taken away by a single loss? Because if all you care about is the outcome, you'll always be at the mercy of external forces. But if you're doing something because you love it, because it fulfills you, then the journey itself is the reward."

"But what if you don't know if you love it anymore?" I asked, more to myself than him.

Dad's face softened. "That's the hardest part, isn't it? Doubt creeps in. You start questioning everything. But the answer doesn't come from giving up. It comes from pushing through, from really listening to yourself. Sometimes, you need to step back and re-evaluate why you started in the first place. Was it for the love of the game? For proving something to others? Or proving something to yourself?"

I thought about Ved, how much he loved cricket but also how much pressure he put on himself. "What if it's both? He loves the game, but he also feels like he has to prove he's good enough."

"That's where the real challenge lies," Dad said, leaning forward. "When you're trying to prove yourself, you're not free. You're always seeking validation from others, whether it's family, friends, or even yourself. True strength comes when you don't need that approval. When you play, or work, or create, simply because it brings you joy, not because it will bring you success."

I nodded slowly, taking it all in. "So... you're saying don't quit, but don't get attached to winning either?"

"Exactly," Dad said, smiling. "Winning is great, but it's not the only thing that matters. Persistence, passion, and personal growth—that's where real success lies. And if Ved can see that, he'll find peace, whether he makes the team or not."

The words from Dad had a way of settling inside me, easing the tension I didn't even realize I had. It wasn't just about solving problems; it was about understanding that not every battle is ours to fight. Sometimes, the best thing we can do is step back, trust those we care about, and give them space to find their own way.

As I left, I knew this wasn't my battle. Ved needed to face his own struggles, frustrations, and dreams. My role was to stand by him, to let him know he wasn't alone. It's his fight, after all. And maybe, just maybe, Dad was right: real growth comes when we let go and trust in the process.

The board exams finally came to an end, and like always, mine went pretty well. There was a sense of relief. Amir, too, said that his exam went well, flashing a proud smile like he had everything under control. As for Ved, he seemed less certain. "I'll pass, I guess," he said with a half- hearted smile, like he was just trying to convince himself. It was clear he'd barely put in the effort at the last minute, scrambling to pull things together in typical Ved fashion.

By the time the results were around the corner, Ved was back to his usual routine, consumed by cricket, while I was neck-deep in JEE preparation. It's strange how life shifts focus so quickly—vibing in the same school, struggling with different fields. One moment you're dreaming of hitting centuries, and the next, you're stuck figuring out whether electrons prefer bonding or roaming free. Career choices have a way of messing with your head like that.

Eventually, all the exams were done and dusted. As for my JEE, it went better than expected, and I couldn't help but give a silent nod of thanks to the sleepless nights in Kota. But if I'm being honest, the real MVP was Ananya's chemistry notes. Without those, I'd probably still be staring at reaction mechanisms like they were some kind of ancient script—though, I love History as well haha.

Then came the wait. Days blurred together, filled with a strange mix of nervous anticipation and empty distractions. I'd replay moments from the exam in my head, but it was mostly just a waiting game. And when the results finally arrived, they came in like a wrecking ball, smashing through the thin veil of hope we'd all been clinging to. Amir's message popped up first: "80% aaye hain bhaiya, I'm happy." A small relief, I thought, at least for him. My own results were in too—I'd topped my school again. The usual pats on the back and congratulatory messages followed, but they felt hollow, like background noise. My mind wasn't there.

It was with Ved.

Then his message appeared. Three words. Short, crushing, and without any escape:

"Fail ho gaya."

I don't know why it hit me so hard. It wasn't my result, but reading those words, it felt like the ground had slipped out from beneath me. My phone stayed in my hand, my eyes glued to the screen as if staring harder would change the outcome. But nothing changed.

I rushed to Ved's house, the familiar streets suddenly feeling alien, weighed down by the thought of what awaited. By the time I reached, the scene inside the Sharma household was anything but calm.

Mr. Sharma, paced the living room like a storm ready to unleash itself. The tension in the room was thick, the kind that made it hard to breathe. The disappointment radiated off him in waves.

"I knew this was going to happen!" he shouted, his voice trembling with frustration. "All that time wasted on cricket! What good has it done now?"

Rima Aunty stood near the doorway, arms crossed, her face a tense mix of anger and hurt. She had been quiet, too quiet. Her anger was a storm waiting to break, held back only by the weight of disappointment.

Then there was Dadi. She sat in the corner, silent, almost invisible, but her presence was loud in its own way. She hadn't spoken a word since the results. Maybe because she had promised Mr. Sharma after Ved's 10th boards that next time would be different. Next time, Ved would do better. But here they were again, and the weight of that unspoken promise was now pressing down on her too.

Radhika didi, stood leaning against the wall, arms folded, her expression unreadable. She was trying hard not to smile, but every now and then, a smirk threatened to break through. She was clearly itching to tease him but knew better than to throw salt in the wound right now. Still, I could see the disappointment in her eyes. Failing the boards was not just a blow to Ved, but to the entire Sharma family.

"This is what all those years of cricket have come to? Fail ho gaya? After everything we've done for you?" Dr. Sharma's voice was shaking now. *"I warned you! I told you to focus on your studies, but no—you wanted to be the next Dhoni, didn't you? Look where that's gotten you, Vedant! You can't even pass your boards! What future do you have now, huh? What are you going to do with this cricket obsession of yours?"*

Ved winced at his father's words, each one hitting him like a punch to the gut. His fists clenched at his sides, but he said nothing. What could he say? He had failed.

From the other side of the room, Radhika didi, leaning against the wall, couldn't resist. Her voice was laced with mock sympathy, though it was clear she wasn't holding back the jab. "Well, well, look who's the genius now. Didn't I tell you, Ved? You can't spend your life chasing a ball around and expect to pass with flying colors. I mean, come on, this is the 12th boards, not some cricket match. I had scored 97% during my time.

She chuckled under her breath, smirking. But even beneath her teasing, there was a hint of disappointment. The Sharma family didn't fail—until now.

Ved's jaw tightened, his frustration boiling over. The mockery, the disappointment, the endless scolding—it was too much. He finally snapped, his voice low and trembling with suppressed anger.

"Enough, Radhika!" His eyes shot up, meeting hers. "You think I don't know what I've done? You think I don't already feel like crap? You don't have to rub it in. You think I wanted this? Do you think I haven't been trying? Cricket is the only thing that makes sense to me, the only thing I'm good at, but I guess none of you will ever understand that!"

Radhika didi's smirk faded, replaced by a look of surprise. Ved, who had always taken her teasing with a grin, now stood before her, raw and wounded.

But before Ved could say anything more, Mr. Sharma's fury exploded.

"Bas! Don't you dare talk back to her! You've lost every right to speak after this failure. You've failed your boards, failed this family, failed yourself! You think cricket is going to save you? What future do you have, Vedant, huh? Look at yourself! Fail ho gaya—you couldn't even do the bare minimum!"

And then, in an instant, it happened.

With a sharp, swift motion, Mr. Sharma's hand flew across Ved's face—a hard slap that echoed through the room, louder than any word that had been said. The impact was harsh, leaving Ved frozen, his cheek stinging, eyes wide with shock.

For a second, the entire room fell silent. Even Radhika didi stopped, her teasing smile completely wiped away. Rima Aunty gasped, her lips trembling, but she held back, anger and heartbreak visible in her eyes. Dadi remained still in her chair, her eyes closing briefly as if she had seen this coming and yet was powerless to stop it.

Ved didn't move. He didn't cry. But the defeat in his eyes was clear. His hand slowly rose to touch the burning mark left on his cheek. His father's words had stung, but this— this was the final blow. The physical manifestation of all the disappointment, frustration, and crushed dreams that had been building up for years.

Taking a shaky breath, Ved slowly looked up, his voice barely a whisper.

"I... I tried..." His words trailed off, heavy with the weight of his failure, but no one seemed to hear him.

Mr. Sharma turned away, his anger still simmering, but the damage had already been done.

BIG CRIME

At that moment, I was at a loss for words. Everything seemed beyond my control. Vedant stood frozen. Mr. Sharma, Rima Aunty, and Radhika didi had already left the room. It was just me, Dadi, and Vedant now.

I stayed there for what seemed like hours, the silence in the room as thick as a heavy fog. The air was cold and unyielding, making the space feel even more oppressive. Vedant stood rooted to the spot, his gaze fixed on the floor, his shoulders slumped as if the weight of the world was pressing down on him. Dadi sat quietly in her chair, her hands folded neatly in her lap, her expression a mixture of contemplation and sorrow. The marks of Mr. Sharma's slap still lingered on Vedant's cheeks, a painful reminder of his recent failure.

The tension in the room was almost palpable, each second stretching into an eternity. My own thoughts were a whirlwind, but I couldn't find the words to break the silence. The clock on the wall ticked relentlessly, each tick a cruel reminder of the passage of time.

Finally, Dadi broke the silence. She took a deep breath, her voice cutting through the heavy atmosphere with unexpected sharpness.

"Well," she began, her tone carrying a mixture of sternness and dry humor, "what's next on the agenda? Giving up on your cricket dreams? Maybe it's time to try something new — like becoming an umpire in the IPL. All you'd have to do is raise your hand and look serious, like the way you are right now."

The words hung in the air, a brief moment of levity in the midst of despair. Vedant's eyes flickered up, his confusion giving way to a hesitant smile. The absurdity of Dadi's suggestion broke through his numbness, and for a brief second, the room was filled with a quiet, almost uncomfortable chuckle. I couldn't help but smile at Dadi's attempt to lighten the mood.

But Dadi wasn't finished. Her eyes softened as she looked at Vedant, her voice steady and filled with warmth. "Look, failing doesn't mean you're done for. It's not the end of the road. If you don't get up and fight now, if you don't find the strength to keep going, then you'll just be a spectator — someone who watches life pass by."

Vedant's expression shifted as he absorbed her words. The humor had cracked the ice, but Dadi's underlying message was clear. The room's atmosphere began to change, the coldness lifting slightly as her words took hold.

Dadi leaned forward, her gaze intense but compassionate. "This isn't about one failure. It's about what you do next. You've got to dust yourself off and prove to yourself — and to everyone else — that you're not done yet. Failure isn't a full stop; it's just a comma in the story of your life."

"I think Dadi's got a point. You've got great knowledge of cricket. Why not try umpiring as a profession? All you need to do is raise your hand and grab the money."

Vedant looked at me with a fierce intensity, as if he might just snap at me. I could almost see him grappling with the idea. If only Radhika didi had been there — she would have enjoyed this moment immensely.

"I think I messed up," Vedant said softly, his voice carrying the weight of regret. "I could've passed if I had just studied a little more at the end. But now... now I regret it. I've wasted two years, and I don't know what to do next!"

"You can keep Amir company now," I said with a chuckle. "Looks like you two will be study buddies from here on."

"I can't face Papa now," Vedant said.

"Regret is a good thing, but living with regret isn't. Face it. Give it some time, and then apologize to your father," Dadi said, her voice calm but firm.

I nodded, agreeing with Dadi's words. She was right—regret couldn't change anything, but facing it might.

Vedant remained silent, his eyes still heavy with the weight of everything, but there was something in his expression that suggested he was beginning to process it all.

As the silence settled back into the room, Dadi stood up slowly. "Now, let's not turn this into a funeral," she said with a hint of her usual dry humor. "You still have a life ahead of you, and it's not over yet."

I chuckled softly, trying to shake off the tension. Vedant didn't say anything, but there was a flicker of determination in his eyes now, a quiet acceptance. Maybe things weren't as broken as they seemed.

Dadi gave Vedant one last look, then turned to me. "Come, we'll give him some time to think."

And with that, we left the room, the weight of the moment lingering behind, but something lighter, a sense of hope, finally breaking through.

Vedant seemed like he'd gone into hibernation. It had been about a week, and I hadn't seen him step out. Honestly, I was even too scared to go to his house and check on him. But finally, one day, Vedant called me, his voice sounding lighter than it had in weeks. "Let's have a chai, bhai. I'm done with my depression."

I chuckled, relieved to hear him sounding like himself again. "About time! I was starting to worry you'd become a philosopher."

"Philosopher?" Vedant scoffed. "After failing my 12th boards, I'm more qualified to become a chaiwala than a philosopher. But yeah, I'm back. Let's go get that tea. Oh, and let's call Amir too. Who knows, maybe I can give him some motivational speech on how to fail gracefully."

I grinned. "Yeah, let's see if you can turn him into a dropout like you."

We met at our usual tea stall, *GCC (Golu Chaiwala Centre)*. *Golu Bhaiya*, the owner, makes the best tea in all of Gomtinagar. As we approached, he gave us a knowing smile. "Arre, Vedant Bhaiya! Back from your 'meditation retreat'?" he teased. "The whole neighborhood's got the memo about your grand failure!"

Vedant rolled his eyes. "Yeah, yeah. Just give us three chais, Golu Bhaiya. I've had enough life lessons for now."

As we sat down, Amir joined us, looking as calm as ever. "What's this? Vedant Bhaiya is out of his cave?"

Vedant smirked. "Out of the cave and straight into enlightenment. I've decided the secret to happiness is chai and cricket. Forget studies."

I laughed. "Well, as long as you don't take up umpiring." "Don't tempt me," Vedant said, sipping his chai. "I'm already imagining myself giving out Dhoni in a match and making history."

I shook my head, grinning. "The only history you'll make is being the first umpire to get chased out of a stadium."

Just as the laughter settled, we heard a commotion. Adnan, Khan chacha's son, came running towards us, panting heavily.

"Amir!" Adnan shouted, breathless. "Your Abba... the police... they've arrested him! He had a fight with Vikki!"

The smiles vanished instantly. Amir's face turned pale, his eyes wide with shock.

Without wasting a second, we rushed towards Siddiqui's house. As we hurried off, Vedant called back, "We'll pay you later, Golu Bhaiya!"

Golu Bhaiya, wiping his hands on his apron, yelled after us, "I'm coming too!"

Vedant barely glanced back, "You better bring the chai then!"

As we arrived at Amir's house, we saw the police vehicle speeding away, its siren still echoing in the distance. Amir shouted, "Abbaaa!" his voice filled with desperation, but there was nothing anyone could do in that moment. The scene felt frozen in time, and we stood there, paralyzed, unable to process what had just happened.

My mind raced, trying to make sense of the chaos. Without thinking, I grabbed my phone and called Dad, quickly explaining everything. He listened calmly and then said firmly, "Head to the police station. I'll meet you there."

With no other plan in sight, I hung up and turned to Vedant and Amir. We knew what had to be done.

"Let's go by scooty"," Vedant suggested, his voice calm but urgent.

Without hesitation, we rushed to his house. Vedant quickly grabbed his scooty, and within moments, we were flying through the streets, the wind whipping against us as we raced toward the police station.

Barely a heartbeat later, we pulled up at the Gomtinagar police station, breathless and anxious, ready to face whatever awaited us.

The three of us walked inside, hearts pounding, as if we were marching straight into a war zone. The faint sound of the ceiling fan creaked overhead, mixing with the distant hum of police chatter. At the front desk, a constable eyed us suspiciously, chewing lazily on a piece of gum.

I saw Dad standing with a constable. We approached him, and he said, "Inspector Vikram Pratap Singh is handling the case," before jerking his thumb towards a door on the left.

We pushed through the door, and there he was. Inspector Vikram Pratap Singh sat behind his desk, his sleeves rolled up, revealing muscular forearms. His eyes, cold and calculating, flicked up as we entered. He had a way of looking at people that made you feel exposed, like he could see straight through you.

"This is all because of Vikki! He's MLA Seenu Chaturvedi's brother, and they must have framed my father!" Amir exclaimed.

Inspector Singh sighed deeply, leaning forward and resting his elbows on the desk. His face, though stern, carried a trace of something more—regret, perhaps. "Look, boy, it's not just about the fight with Vikki. There's something much bigger at play here."

We froze. I felt a knot tighten in my stomach as the inspector's tone shifted to something more serious, more secretive.

"Your father," Singh began, his voice low, "isn't just being held for a street brawl. A few years ago, a case was filed against him. Seenu Chaturvedi accused your father of killing his sister."

There was a pause so heavy, I thought time had stopped.

"His sister?" Amir whispered, the disbelief clear in his voice. "You mean... my mother?"

Inspector Singh nodded gravely. "Yes. But we couldn't find any solid evidence back then. The case was buried. Seenu wasn't MLA at that time, so your father managed to survive the accusations."

As if on cue, the door to the office creaked open, and in walked Seenu Chaturvedi himself, flanked by his brother Vikki and a couple of local bodyguards. The air thickened with tension, as though every molecule in the room shifted under the weight of their presence.

Seenu strode in with a quiet authority, his eyes locking onto Amir with a cold gaze. "But now," he said, his voice dripping with malice, "he won't escape."

Vikki, nursing his injuries, sat down next to his brother, wincing theatrically as he pointed to his bruises. "Look at what that man did to me, Inspector. It's a clear case of assault."

Inspector Singh, maintaining his composure, offered them both chairs and asked for chai. The contrast between the calmness of the request and the storm brewing in the room felt almost surreal.

Seenu turned to my dad, who had accompanied us, his expression shifting from venomous to something more respectful. "Srivastav ji," Seenu began, "you're a well-respected man in this area. I appreciate that. But I advise you not to get involved in matters you don't fully understand."

My dad, always the composed one, nodded respectfully. "Seenu ji, I understand your position, but the injuries don't seem severe enough to involve the police. Can't we resolve this matter differently?"

Seenu leaned forward, his face hardening again. "This isn't just about a few bruises, Srivastav ji. This man—Siddiqui— destroyed my family. He convinced my innocent sister to marry him, despite our objections, and then he killed her. He's a monster. And if you think that's the worst of it, you're mistaken. He also killed my niece, Fatima. Do you really think she took poison on her own?"

Amir shook his head, eyes welling up. "No... Abba wouldn't..."

"Abba wouldn't what?" Seenu snapped, cutting him off. "Your father is a criminal, Amir. You're blinded by your loyalty, but that doesn't change the truth."

Inspector Singh cleared his throat, cutting in. "There are numerous cases against your father, Amir. His past... it's darker than you know."

Vikki chimed in, a smirk playing on his lips. "He was in politics too, wasn't he, bhaiya? Back when he was a youth leader in the Muslim League?"

Seenu nodded. "Yes. Back then, the party was in control of the state. Your father, Amir, he committed plenty of crimes under their banner. And now... it's my turn to make sure he pays for them."

Amir's voice cracked, barely able to contain the emotion. "Abba couldn't do this. He can't be the man you're saying he is."

Seenu sneered, "Believe what you want, boy, but the truth will always come out. Your father's time is up."

The room fell into a heavy silence. The weight of Seenu's words lingered in the air, and for the first time, Amir looked truly lost—caught between the father he knew and the accusations that threatened to destroy him.

The weight of the revelations from the police station was heavy as we left. Dad suggested we consult a lawyer to handle the complex legal situation.

"I'll arrange for a lawyer to meet us tomorrow," Dad said. "We need professional help to navigate this."

Amir, suddenly spoke up, his voice barely above a whisper. "I want to see Abba."

Amir, with a heavy heart, asked to go back inside alone. We understood his need for privacy and decided to wait outside.

After about half an hour, Amir emerged. His face was pale, and his eyes were wide with shock and exhaustion. He looked like he had been through an emotional storm, his shoulders slumped and his steps heavy.

Seeing him, we rushed over. "Amir, what happened? Are you okay?" I asked, my voice tinged with concern.

Amir barely glanced at us as he stumbled toward the exit. "I... I don't know what to say," he muttered, his voice strained. "I'm... I'm shocked. I didn't expect it to be like this."

I looked at Dad, who nodded in understanding. "Let's get out of here. We need to regroup and figure out our next steps.

"Abba told me the truth..." Amir's voice trembled as he spoke. "He admitted... he killed Ammi."

I stood frozen, barely able to process what Amir had just said. Dad, too, was silent, his eyes wide with disbelief.

"I asked him why," Amir continued, his voice cracking. "At first, he refused to explain, but then... he finally told me. He said that when he was the leader of the Muslim League, marrying Ammi—Seenu's sister—was all part of a political move, a calculated plan to gain influence. But later, when his party collapsed, everything fell apart. He couldn't handle it anymore."

Amir paused, struggling to hold back tears. "He said he lost control. His anger... it got the best of him, and he... he hurt her." Amir's voice broke. "But he swore he never touched Fatima. He said, 'I didn't do anything to her.'"

There was a long silence as the weight of his words sank in. "Then, he just told me to leave," Amir whispered. "'Focus on your life and work. Leave this behind,' he said. That's all."

The silence that followed was suffocating. The weight of Amir's words hung in the air, as if the world had shifted beneath our feet, leaving us with more questions than answers.

"Then there's no point in hiring a lawyer," Vedant said.

Dad looked at Amir, "We'll talk to the lawyer tomorrow and see what can be done," he said.

It was an absolutely insane day. The more I thought about it, the more I felt overwhelmed. Just as we were trying to get through Vedant's family drama, Amir's entire world collapsed. That night, Amir stayed over with me. I felt terrible for him, though I could never fully understand what he was going through. How could anyone, really? Life can be so cruel sometimes. One moment we were laughing over Golu Bhaiya's chai, and now this? It was all just so messed up.

The next day, Dad trying to figure out what our next steps would be with the lawyer. The tension was suffocating, and it felt like time had slowed to a crawl.

Suddenly, Dad's phone rang, and his face instantly changed as he listened to the person on the other end. His eyes widened, and he stood up abruptly.

"What happened, Dad?" I asked, feeling a pit form in my stomach.

He hesitated for a moment, glancing at Amir before he spoke, his voice low and heavy. "Mr. Siddiqui... he's dead."

The room fell into complete silence. Amir froze, his face pale, unable to process the words. I saw his lips tremble as he tried to form a response, but nothing came out. The shock hit all of us like a wave, and for a moment, we just stood there, paralyzed.

Without a second thought, we rushed out of the house, hurrying towards the police station. The ride was a blur— none of us spoke. My heart pounded in my chest, and I could only imagine what Amir was going through, sitting beside me, wiped of any expression.

When we arrived, Amir stumbled out of the car, barely able to walk. His legs gave out for a second, but he steadied himself, refusing help. His eyes were wide, still processing the reality of what had just happened. We pushed through the doors of the station, and Amir collapsed into a chair, silent tears streaming down his face.

None of us knew what to say. How could we?

Inspector Singh, standing with a grave expression as he saw us approach.

Without saying a word, he gestured for us to follow him. I could feel the weight of the moment in every step we took.

It was like walking through a nightmare we couldn't wake up from.

We were led into a back room, where the body of Mr. Siddiqui lay covered under a white sheet. The silence was suffocating as Inspector Singh pulled it back just enough for us to see. Amir's breath caught in his throat, and for a second, I thought he might pass out.

"I'm sorry for your loss," Inspector Singh began, his voice steady but filled with a strange mix of regret and professionalism. "He tried to escape from custody earlier this Morning."

Amir's head snapped toward him, his eyes wide with disbelief. "Escape?" His voice was barely a whisper, shaky and broken. "How? Why would he—"

Inspector Singh cut him off gently but firmly. "We had no choice. He resisted, and we had to respond. It was an unwanted situation, but in the end... it became an encounter."

"An encounter?" I couldn't hold back the disbelief in my voice. "You killed him?"

The inspector's face tightened, his eyes meeting each of ours. "I understand how this looks, but your father... he was involved in much more than just a simple fight, Amir. There were cases. Dark things in his past. We were hoping to get him to cooperate, but he made a move to flee. We had to act, or... it could've been much worse."

My voice cracked as I tried to make sense of it all. "But, Inspector... how could it come to this? It doesn't add up."

Inspector Singh sighed deeply. "I wish it hadn't. We didn't want this outcome, but his past caught up to him. There were accusations—serious ones. Murder. Manipulation. But without solid proof, it was all hearsay. Still, tonight, he acted in desperation."

Amir looked up, his face pale and gaunt. "He said... he said I wouldn't understand. But I—" His voice broke, and he fell silent, tears slipping down his face.

We all stood there, helpless, as the reality of what had happened sank in. There were no words to soothe Amir, no explanations to make sense of the chaos. We had come looking for answers, but all we found was a painful truth, one that none of us were ready to accept.

CHAPTER NINE

THE DISRESPECTED WALK

"Good riddance, I say," a rough voice muttered from the edge of the crowd, the speaker looking at Siddiqui's lifeless body. "The man was a mess—killed his own wife. Lucky the inspector shot him."

Amir tensed beside me, his fists clenched, but he said nothing.

We stood in the graveyard, the wind blowing gently through the trees as a quiet crowd gathered around. The ground felt as heavy as the words in the air.

Another voice, harsher and louder, cut through the murmurs. "A monster, that's what he was. Manipulated his daughter, molested her. It's a relief he's gone."

The crowd showed no mercy, their whispers growing louder, each word cutting deeper into Amir. I could feel him falling apart beside me, his chest rising and falling fast, but he stayed silent, trembling.

I looked at Amir, still crumpled by the graveside, his shoulders shaking with grief. This wasn't just about the loss of his father. It was the destruction of everything Amir thought he knew.

And there, in the midst of it all, Siddiqui's body lay cold and silent—his life, his name, now drowned beneath the venom of the crowd's curses.

As we were leaving the graveyard, the weight of everything heavy on our minds, Dad placed a hand on Amir's shoulder. His voice was soft, filled with genuine care. "Amir, why don't you come and live with us? You don't have to go through this alone. Our home is open for you, for as long as you need."

Amir, eyes still red from the pain and exhaustion, shook his head gently. "I appreciate it, Uncle. But I need to stay at my place. I need to figure things out on my own now."

Dad sighed, his expression understanding yet concerned. "I understand, beta. But remember, if you need anything— anything at all—don't hesitate to reach out. We're always here for you."

Amir nodded, managing a small, grateful smile.

Me and Ved began visiting Amir regularly, bringing him food and checking in on him, though each visit seemed to weigh heavier than the last.

One evening, as we were walking by Raza Masjid,

"There goes the murderer's son," one of them sneered loud enough for Amir to hear. "Like father, like son. Who knows what he'll do next?"

A woman walking past with her child clutched the little boy's hand tighter, her eyes narrowing at Amir. "Stay away from him," she muttered to the child. "His blood is tainted."

Another man, crossing the street, spat on the ground as he saw Amir. "You think we've forgotten?" he barked. "Your Abba may be gone, but don't think we won't keep an eye on you. You're next."

Someone from a nearby shop shouted, "Why are you still here? You think we'll buy eggs from the son of a killer? Your family should've left long ago!"

His small egg shop, once a bustling corner of the community, became a ghost of itself. Customers stopped coming. People went out of their way to avoid him, as if he carried the same curse they believed had destroyed his family.

A teenager, emboldened by the crowd, called out mockingly, "Hey, murderer's son! Maybe you'll follow in your father's footsteps, huh? You gonna finish the job he started?"

Amir clenched his fists but said nothing, his gaze fixed on the ground as the insults kept coming. One older man, his face twisted in disgust, shouted from across the street, "There's no place for people like you here! You're cursed, boy. It's only a matter of time before you bring more ruin."

As we walked toward Amir's house, the insults from earlier still hung heavy in the air.

"I need to go Bhaiya," Amir muttered, barely loud enough for us to hear.

Before we could respond, he bolted. Without a glance back, he turned sharply and started running.

"What the—Amir!" Ved shouted, immediately chasing after him.

I looked at Ved, confused. "Where's he going?"

"I don't know!" Ved panted, sprinting ahead.

We chased him through narrow lanes, dodging pedestrians, nearly tripping over stray dogs. Amir was fast, his feet pounding the pavement harder with each step, like he was running from something much deeper than just us.

I struggled to keep up, calling out between breaths, "Amir! Wait! What the hell, man?"

He didn't slow down. If anything, he seemed to pick up speed, darting down unfamiliar streets. Ved and I exchanged a worried glance as we ran. This wasn't a random run—he was heading somewhere with purpose.

As we rounded a corner, it hit me. I grabbed Ved's arm. "He's heading toward the river, isn't he?"

Ved's eyes widened in realization. "Damn it. The Gomti."

When we finally reached the riverbank, Amir was already at the edge, staring out over the dark waters, his back turned to us. The current shimmered under the moonlight, but there was a heaviness in the air, a stillness that chilled me to the bone.

"Amir!" I called out, breathless. "What are you doing?"

Amir didn't turn around, his body stiff, like he was trapped in some invisible fight.

Ved cautiously stepped forward, his voice steady but soft. "Amir, come on, man. What's going on?"

"I... I can't tolerate anymore," Amir's voice cracked.

Ved exchanged a quick look with me, then tried again, his tone lighter but serious. "Look, people can be real jerks, okay? But that doesn't mean you have to listen to them. You're not your father, and no one—no one—has the right to define you."

Amir looked down, his breathing heavy but slowing. "I don't know what to do."

Ved nodded towards the distance. "First, we're going to Dadi's. She'll know what to say. Chai, parathas, and wisdom—guaranteed to fix everything."

Ved carefully put a hand on Amir's shoulder, his voice gentle but firm. "You're not alone in this, Amir. Dadi always gives the best advice to me, no matter how messed up things get. She'll know what to say to you too. Trust me."

We walked in silence back to Ved's house, the weight of the insults and the near breakdown hanging heavy in the air. By the time we reached the front door, Amir looked worn out, like every step had drained what little energy he had left.

Dadi sat on the porch, as she did every evening, her wrinkled hands slowly turning the beads of her mala. The soft chants of "Om Namah Shivaya" escaped her lips, blending with the golden light of the setting sun. The peace of the evening seemed unshakable, as if the world had momentarily paused in reverence to her stillness.

The three of us approached her slowly, not wanting to disturb her moment of quiet. She noticed us before we could speak, her eyes glimmering with a knowing look.

Ved spoke first. "Dadi, Amir has been through a lot. He's been judged for things he didn't do, and people are refusing to see who he truly is. We've tried everything, but nothing seems to work. He needs your advice."

Dadi's eyes softened as she looked at Amir, who was fidgeting nervously, his gaze cast downward.

She nodded, her fingers gently tracing the beads in her hand as she listened quietly while we told her everything— the harsh words, the societal refusal, Amir's silent suffering.

Once we finished, she sat in silence for a moment, her eyes closed as if drawing wisdom from deep within herself, or perhaps from Lord Shiva.

Finally, she spoke, her voice calm yet full of depth. "Societal refusal," she began, "is one of the biggest attacks on the heart. It's like a wound that bleeds endlessly."

Amir nodded.

"But," Dadi continued, her lips curving into a light smile, "don't take it on your heart. Take it on your ego. That's probably better," she said with a glimmer of humor, making us chuckle despite the heaviness of the moment.

"However," she added, her voice growing serious again, "sometimes the best thing a person can do is focus on spiritual gain. *When no one listens, the Mighty listens.*"

Amir looked confused.

"Beta, it's your choice how you react to this. It's your journey to gain the respect of others. Look at my Ved, for instance," she said, nodding toward her grandson. "He is a hero."

"I can only suggest one thing," she said, her tone soft but steady. "You can go somewhere... away from all this noise. Maybe even my city. Kashi."

"Kashi?" Amir asked, surprised.

Dadi nodded, her eyes distant, filled with memories. "Yes, Kashi. It's my lord's city. I've learned a lot from that sacred place, and perhaps, you too can find something meaningful there. Disconnect from the people who judge you. Sometimes, the way to gain respect is to first find yourself."

We exchanged glances, the weight of her suggestion sinking in.

"Kashi is a place of spiritual context and inner power," she continued. "Go there for a few years, leave behind the ones who refuse you. In that distance, you may find the strength to return—stronger, more whole—and regain the respect you deserve."

Amir's face softened, the idea of retreating to Kashi slowly taking root.

Dadi reached over and placed her hand on Amir's, the gesture both comforting and firm. "Remember, beta, *the world outside may refuse you, but the world within you holds the power to shape who you become. Seek that power. It will guide you back.*"

For the first time that day, Amir looked up with a sense of purpose.

"May my Shiv Ji and Ganga Mata bless you with the purpose you need," she said softly, her eyes fixed on Amir. "You are free now, beta. Probably the luckiest of all. Very few are as lucky to be this free—you have no family to weigh you down with emotions. This freedom is your gift."

Amir listened intently, his expression thoughtful.

"And I'm sure that Varanasi's food will attract you," she added with a twinkle in her eye, lightening the mood, "but don't stay there too long. Remember, you have to gain respect, not to linger."

Amir sat quietly after Dadi's words, as if her advice had planted a seed of clarity within him. He glanced at me, uncertainty still flickering in his eyes, but I could see the decision forming in his heart. Dadi's words had reached him deeply. It was in the way he sat straighter, in the way his hand stopped fidgeting, in the way he finally exhaled a breath he had been holding for too long.

"I think I'll do it," Amir finally said, his voice quiet but firm. "I'll go to Kashi. Maybe... maybe Dadi's right. Maybe that's what I need."

Ved and I exchanged looks, both of us feeling a mix of relief and concern. Kashi was far, and the thought of being without Amir, even for a while, weighed on us. But at the same time, it felt like the right thing for him.

After a long silence, I couldn't help but think of Dad. He had always been practical, grounded—maybe he could offer more help to Amir in this journey.

"I'll talk to Dad," I said, standing up from the porch. "He'll know what to do."

Amir nodded.

Later that night, I found Dad in the living room, sipping tea and reading the evening paper. The soft clinking of the cup against the saucer was the only sound in the otherwise quiet house.

I stood in the doorway for a moment, unsure of how to begin, but then the words spilled out.

"Dad, can we talk for a second?"

He looked up from his paper, his eyes immediately softening when he saw my expression. "Of course, beta. What's on your mind?"

I sat down beside him and explained everything—Dadi's advice, Amir's decision, his struggles, and how Kashi seemed like the answer.

Dad listened carefully, nodding as I spoke, his usual calm presence making me feel like everything would be okay. When I finished, there was a long pause as he thought about it.

Finally, he spoke. "If Amir feels that Kashi is where he needs to be, then we should support him. And if he's going there, he should also focus on his education, he can continue his secondary education. It will give him a sense of purpose and structure while he seeks spiritual growth."

He smiled, placing a hand on my shoulder. "Don't worry, I'll take care of his needs in Varanasi. We'll make sure he's comfortable there.

The following morning was bittersweet. The sun was just starting to rise as Amir prepared to leave. The house felt different, quieter than usual, as if it, too, was preparing for his departure. Dad had already made arrangements for Amir's stay in Varanasi—everything from accommodation to finances, and had also looked into educational opportunities for him.

As the car pulled up in front of the house, Ved and I stood with Amir, the silence between us thick with unspoken words. Amir was carrying a small bag, enough for a few clothes and books—he didn't need much. His journey to Kashi wasn't about possessions; it was about finding something deeper.

Dad appeared at the doorway, his expression soft but serious. He walked over to Amir and placed a firm hand on his shoulder.

"Go, beta," Dad said, his voice a mix of warmth and mock sternness. "You've got your work cut out for you. Not just finding spiritual peace, but also hitting the books. You'll be continuing your secondary education there. Might as well get two birds with one stone."

Amir looked up, a small smile playing at his lips. "Thank you, Uncle. I don't know what to say..."

As the driver closed the trunk and Amir climbed into the back seat, I tried to keep my voice steady.

"Take care, man," I said.

Amir looked at both of us. "I'll be back soon, Bhaiya with a purpose," Amir said.

As the car disappeared down the road, leaving a trail of dust, Ved and I stood there, watching it go.

CHAPTER TEN

PERFECT LIFE

And just then, my phone rang...

"Ananya!?" I said, my eyes widening as her name appeared on the screen.

Ved leaned in with a mischievous grin and asked, "Who's this Ananya, my boy?"

I felt my face turn red, and in my flustered state, I forgot Dad was standing right next to us.

"Pick up the phone, or Ananya might think you're stuck in a secret mission," Dad said with a laugh before walking away, leaving me to handle the awkwardness and the ringing phone.

As soon as I picked up the phone, the sweetest and most melodic sound filled my ears.

"Hiieeee..."

I could hardly contain my blush, and Ved wasn't any better —he was practically grinning from ear to ear as he watched me.

"Hi," I managed to reply, trying to sound cool. "How are you?"

"I'm good. How about you?" Ananya asked.

"Me too, great," I replied, trying to keep my composure.

"You completely forgot about me, huh?" Ananya said playfully.

"Not at all, I was—" I started to say but got stuck, unable to finish my sentence.

Meanwhile, Ved looked like he was enjoying the conversation even more than I was.

Then Ananya asked, "So, how much did you score?" "Scored?" I stammered, completely caught off guard.

"Haven't you heard? The JEE Mains results just got declared!" Ananya said with a mix of excitement and surprise.

"What? Really?" I responded, completely taken aback. "I had no idea about it!"

"Let me check my results, then. I'll call you later," I said quickly, my mind racing. "Byyeee!"

I hung up the phone and rushed toward my room.

"Hey, boy! Who's this Ananya? Tell me first!" Ved shouted, chasing after me.

I quickly turned on my laptop and headed to the results website. Ved, seeing what was going on, crossed his fingers and grinned. "Looks like we might be celebrating soon," he said. "Get ready for a party!"

"hope so"

The website stubbornly refused to load, heightening the sense of anticipation with each passing moment. When it finally opened, the results appeared on the screen: 99.5845022 percentile, CRL - 4900.

A wave of disbelief and exhilaration washed over as the numbers registered. The hard work and late nights had culminated in this moment of triumph.

Ved, watching the result unfold, couldn't contain his excitement. His eyes widened, and a broad smile spread across his face. "I knew it!" he exclaimed, his voice full of joy. "We're definitely celebrating!"

I knew my result would be good, so I wasn't overly surprised, but cracking the JEE was still a tremendous achievement for me. Achieving what you set out to do is truly the best feeling in the world.

The congratulations seemed to come from every corner— my dad beamed with pride, my teachers sent their well wishes, and the entire neighborhood buzzed with excitement. Ananya was one of the first to reach out, and even Ved's family showered me with praises. As I went to deliver laddoos to Mr. Sharma, his appreciation was unlike anything I'd ever experienced. He spoke to me with a level of admiration I'd never seen him give Vedant.

Dadi, with her gentle smile, placed her hands on my head and blessed me, her pride evident in her eyes. Rima Aunty insisted I sit down and enjoy her famous aaloo parathas, the smell of which brought a wave of comfort and warmth. And then, Radhika didi came over with the most thoughtful gift I could have imagined—For the Love of Physics by Walter Lewin, a book that she knew would mean the best to me.

It felt like I was living in the prime of my life, surrounded by love, appreciation, and the sweet taste of success. Every moment seemed filled with the warmth of accomplishment and the joy of those who had been part of my journey.

"Thanks, didi," I said gracefully, holding the book with a smile.

She smiled back, her eyes warm. "There's a lot to learn from you," she said thoughtfully. "You always follow what makes you happy, just like my little bhai." She nodded toward Ved, who was standing nearby, probably sensing another teasing remark. "I may tease him, but I truly appreciate individuality and personal choice. I'm really glad to see that in you. Keep that spirit alive."

She paused for a moment and then, with a playful glint in her eyes, added, "And you know what? Come on, let's have Mumma's parathas, and then I'll tell you something."

With that, we all headed to the hall, anticipation rising again—not for results this time, but for whatever Radhika didi had in store.

"I started a campaign," Radhika didi said, taking a bite of the delicious aaloo paratha.

I paused, intrigued. "A campaign?" I asked, curious about what she was up to.

"Yeah, about liberty," Radhika didi said, her tone shifting as she took another bite of paratha.

"Liberty?" I repeated, now fully intrigued.

She nodded, her eyes brightening. "It's a campaign I've been working on—focused on personal freedom. It's about encouraging people, especially the younger generation, to make their own choices and not feel trapped by society's expectations. Whether it's career, lifestyle, or even small everyday decisions, people deserve to live life on their own terms."

Her words struck a chord. She looked over at Ved, then back at me. "You two are great examples of that. You both follow what makes you happy, despite all the pressure around you. That's the message I want to spread— embracing the freedom to be yourself."

As she spoke, I could sense the depth of her passion for the campaign. It wasn't just about making a statement; it was about empowering people to live authentically. The idea felt powerful, and I admired how much it aligned with what we had been striving for in our own lives.

"India is already a liberal country, my daughter," Mr. Sharma said, approaching us with a slight waddle and his heavy belly swaying with each step. "Haven't you read the Constitution?"

"I don't think so, Papa," didi replied, her voice firm. *"In terms of liberalism, communism, and secularism, it's all just political noise across India. The real issue is whether we're actually thinking independently or if we're just being forced into certain ways of thinking. It's like we're trapped in a cycle where genuine freedom of thought is hard to come by."*

"Do whatever you want," Mr. Sharma said. "I'm already done with the boy," he added, glancing at Ved with a hint of frustration. "I guess I won't expect much from you either."

Then, without warning, Ved, who had been quiet until this moment, stood up abruptly, pushing his plate aside with a forceful gesture. His face was flushed with anger as he spoke, his voice carrying a mix of hurt and frustration. *"Sometimes I seriously think about leaving this house,"* he said, his words laced with bitterness. "It feels like there's no real value for me here, no matter what I do. I'm just tired of feeling like I don't matter."

And with that, Ved turned and walked away, his frustration evident in every step he took. I thought about getting up and leaving too, but Radhika didi gave me a subtle glance, signaling me to stay and enjoy the paratha.

I didn't feel like I'd actually be able to enjoy the paratha after everything that had just happened. But as I tried to continue eating, a loud, infectious laugh echoed from the doorway. It was Gauri Aunty—Vedant's Bua and Mr. Sharma's sister—making her way in with heavy, deliberate steps. Her entrance seemed almost like a family tradition. I couldn't help but imagine Vedant at her age, and it brought a chuckle to my lips.

Gauri Aunty had kajal smudged around her eyes, and her cheeks were an exact replica of Mr. Sharma's. Her mouth was stretched into a smile so wide, it looked like she could devour ten parathas in one go. She carried a box of sweets in her hands, which only added to the surprise.

I was taken aback. Why was Gauri Aunty here to celebrate my success? She hadn't even celebrated Vedant's achievements.

But what's this? Gauri Aunty hadn't come alone. Right behind her was Pranjal, her son and Vedant's cousin. Pranjal was dressed to impress, with a garland hanging around his neck and a broad smile stretching across his face, resembling a joyous, plump parrot.

"Namaste, Bhaiya," Gauri Aunty greeted Mr. Sharma with a warm smile, her voice carrying a mix of enthusiasm and an almost theatrical flourish. She extended a box of laddus towards him. "Here, have some sweets!"

Mr. Sharma looked up, a bit puzzled but nonetheless accepting the gesture. Gauri Aunty opened the box and, with an exaggerated flourish, began feeding him the sweets with her own hands. It was a sight that could have been straight out of a melodramatic film, complete with the background score of a triumph.

Radhika didi greeted her with a polite nod, and I followed suit, attempting to mask my own curiosity. It was clear that Gauri Aunty's visit was more than just a casual drop-in.

And then, without warning, Gauri Aunty launched into a monologue that left me and didi's ears ringing. "You won't believe it," she started, her voice filled with a mixture of pride and barely-contained glee. "Pranjal has cracked the JEE Mains! Yes, my Pranjal! He's done it!"

As she spoke, her eyes sparkled with a satisfaction that could only come from having outdone someone—or in this case, everyone. Her voice grew louder, almost as if she wanted to make sure that every single person in the neighborhood knew about her son's achievement.

"Pranjal, come here and greet everyone!" she called, and in walked Pranjal, looking like he had just stepped out of a fashion magazine. He was decked out in a shiny garland, which hung around his neck like he was the guest of honor at a grand celebration. His face was lit up with a smile so wide, it seemed to stretch from ear to ear, giving him the appearance of a joyous parrot.

"Namaste, Mama!" Pranjal chirped, nodding to Mr. Sharma, who had now become the audience to this impromptu performance.

Mr. Sharma gave a nod of approval and offered his warm congratulations to Pranjal.

Rima Aunty, who had been observing quietly from the corner, couldn't hide her annoyance. It was clear she wasn't thrilled about all the attention Gauri Aunty and Pranjal were getting. After all, Rima Aunty's own child was still in 11th grade, making the contrast with Pranjal's achievement all the more glaring.

Dadi, as usual, was the picture of calm, her eyes twinkling with a mixture of amusement and wisdom. She had seen more family drama than anyone could count.

"Well, well, Gauri, this is a surprise!" Rima Aunty said with a tight smile, her tone attempting to mask her irritation. "I didn't realize Pranjal had achieved such a milestone."

"Oh, absolutely!" Gauri Aunty replied, her smile almost too bright. "Pranjal has done exceptionally well. I thought I'd bring some sweets to celebrate his success!"

As she spoke, her gaze flickered over to me and then back to Rima Aunty. It was clear her visit wasn't just about the sweets. It was a subtle display of Pranjal's success, a not- so-subtle nudge to Rima Aunty.

"Well, isn't that just wonderful," Rima Aunty said through gritted teeth. "I'm sure Vedant will make us proud someday too."

"Of course, of course," Gauri Aunty replied, her tone dripping with feigned sincerity. "But for now, let's enjoy these sweets and bask in Pranjal's glory!"

As the conversation continued, it became clear that Gauri Aunty's visit was more than just a friendly gesture. It was a carefully orchestrated performance to showcase Pranjal's success while gently reminding everyone, especially Rima Aunty, of her son's achievement.

Gauri Aunty, with a grin that bordered on smug, turned to Rima Aunty and said, "Rima, I must say, it's impressive how you manage to keep the family so busy. Making Vedant's tiffin every day must feel like a full-time job in itself! Haha!"

Rima Aunty's face flushed, her smile faltering as she tried to mask her embarrassment. "Oh, well, you know, *every child has their own pace.*"

Gauri Aunty's eyes sparkled with a hint of mischief. "Indeed! But it's really something to see how Pranjal has already cracked JEE Mains. It's a shame when we have to wait so long to see results from others, don't you think?"

The room fell silent for a moment as everyone processed Gauri Aunty's pointed remark. Rima Aunty's cheeks turned a deeper shade of red as she struggled to find a response.

Vedant, who had been silently listening to the exchange, could no longer contain his frustration. With a mix of anger and hurt, he retreated to his room, his footsteps heavy with disappointment.

I tried to follow him, but Radhika Didi placed a hand on my shoulder. "I'll take care of him," she said softly. "You go on. You need to focus on cracking JEE Advance too. And, please, try to score better than this parrot," she added, nodding toward Pranjal with a smirk in her eyes.

I glanced at Pranjal, who was basking in the praise, and then back to Radhika Didi. I nodded and headed off, determined to push through the awkwardness and focus on what really mattered.

I didn't know what further drama might have unfolded within the Sharma family, but I was certainly concerned about Vedant. However, I had full faith that Radhika Didi would support him completely. So, I focused on preparing for JEE Advance in the coming days.

It was incredibly challenging, but somehow, I managed to keep my mind in check. And the result made it all worth the effort—*I cracked JEE Advanced too, with a CRL of 2319!* Tears welled up in my eyes—tears of relief, pride, and sheer joy. Against all odds, I had done it. I had cracked the exam, and in that moment, it felt like the world had shifted in my favor.

My dad, being an alumnus of IIT Delhi, naturally advised me to follow in his footsteps. He had always spoken so fondly of his time there, and I could see the pride in his eyes when he suggested that I consider IIT Delhi as my first choice. However, despite the legacy and prestige that came with it, I had to respectfully decline. "Dad, I'm not getting Electrical Engineering there," I explained. It wasn't just about following in his footsteps; it was about following my own path. Electrical Engineering had always fascinated me, especially my deep interest in quantum mechanics. The intricacies of the subject captured my imagination in a way that few things could.

After much thought, I chooses IIT Jodhpur. It wasn't the biggest or most famous IIT, but it offered the branch I was passionate about. And there was another, somewhat personal reason for choosing Jodhpur. I'm sure you can guess what it was—yes, it was partly because of Ananya. A while ago, she had casually mentioned that I should visit Jaipur, her hometown, someday. And as fate would have it, IIT Jodhpur was the closest IIT to Jaipur. The idea of being near her, even if only geographically, gave me a little extra nudge in that direction. So, in the end, it wasn't just my academic interest that guided my decision—it was the hope of keeping some connections alive, however subtle.

"When I excitedly told Vedant about my result, I expected a genuine smile, maybe a hint of the old cheer we used to share. But when I saw a flicker of something else in his eyes —envy, maybe even jealousy—or perhaps I was wrong."

"Hey, Ved," I started, leaning against the doorframe of his room. "I cracked JEE Advanced. Got a CRL of 2319." I tried to sound casual, though a part of me hoped for some sort of congratulation.

Ved looked up from where he sat, his gaze intense but distant. "That's great," he said, his voice flat, devoid of any real excitement. "Really, it is." His tone, though polite, was edged with something I couldn't quite put my finger on.

I was about to thank him when he added, his voice colder, *"But you know, sometimes, it feels like you're just living this... perfect life."* He stood up, brushing past me as he began to pace the room, clearly agitated. "Look at you. Everything you do, you just... make it. You succeed. It's like there's nothing you can't do."

"Ved, it's not about competition," I said. "This was never about us competing. We're friends. Brothers, even. I'm not racing against you."

"Who said I was competing?" Vedant stopped pacing and turned to face me, his eyes narrowing. "I don't need to compete with you. I already know I'm better."

"Then why do you sound so bitter?" I asked, trying to keep my voice steady.

He let out a bitter laugh, his shoulders sagging slightly. "You just don't get it, do you?" he said, shaking his head. "Look at yourself. Have you ever faced a real problem? Have you ever felt tortured by these endless family conflicts, the constant pressure to be something more than you are?"

I could hear the weight of his words, the exhaustion behind them. I stayed quiet, letting him vent.

"See me? I'm still stuck in 11th, miles behind you. And no matter how hard I try, I keep falling short. It's like... you're always just ahead, unreachable. While I'm here, drowning in all this... this mess." He gestured vaguely around him, but I knew what he meant. The family, the expectations, the disappointments. "I know you worked hard for this, but sometimes, it feels like everything just... falls into place for you. Like you're made for a Perfect Life."

For a moment, the room felt still, like something had shifted between us. I stood there, letting Vedant's words sink in. Maybe he was right—my life did seem perfect.

I thought to myself, if Vedant had been in my place, he might have cleared the exam too. And if I were in his position, perhaps I would've felt left behind as well. Then I considered others. If only Hriday didn't have so much family tension, he might be here with us. If Vishal hadn't faced financial struggles, he could've chased his dreams. And if Abhishek hadn't given up on himself, his life might have turned out differently.

"Life isn't perfect for any of us," I said. "It's the circumstances that shape our paths. Maybe you're not seeing it right now, but we're all fighting our own battles."

"I'm just done, bhai," Vedant said.

CHAPTER ELEVEN

The Last Inning

Vedant was completely shattered. His U-19 and zonal selection matches were approaching, but for the first time, I had doubts about him. I wasn't sure what he would do. In a month, I was leaving for Jodhpur to start my next chapter, and I couldn't figure out how to help him. He was so uncertain about his career.

Finally, after a long silence, I turned to him and said, **"I've got your back. Not just now, but always."**

But his response shook me. He looked straight at me and said, "Exactly! You are always. And who am I? What's my identity? A failure? A loser? Stupid? I don't even know if I'm right or wrong anymore. But my dreams... they mean everything to me. They don't get it—especially Doctor Sahab.

"It's okay if the world thinks I'm a failure, a loser. But Bhai, My father?" His voice broke a little. "I just wish he would come to watch me bat once. *I want to show my father that I'm the best in my business.*"

"You know," Vedant said, his voice trembling, "this is going to be my last....." He trailed off, unable to finish the thought.

Last? I said.

"My last inning," Vedant continued. "If I don't make it, I don't think I'll be able to play cricket anymore."

The Silenced continued.

On the day of the match, Vedant was eager for Mr. Sharma to come and watch him play, but he hadn't mentioned anything directly to him. So, I asked Radhika Didi to try and convince Mr. Sharma to attend Vedant's match. She agreed to speak with him, hoping to persuade him to go.

However, she wasn't able to change his mind. Mr. Sharma told her that he would only come to watch if Vedant could show him something impressive, like a good result. He questioned why Vedant hadn't played at any notable level if he was truly deserving. The disappointment was clear in his response, and it was evident that he needed more than just words to be convinced.

"I'm going to the match today. I want to be there to support Vedant," Dadi declared firmly.

Rima Aunty, glancing anxiously from the window of the kitchen, tried to reason with her. "Amma, it's really hot outside. The sun's rays could be too harsh for you, and watching a cricket match in the afternoon can be exhausting."

But Dadi was undeterred. "I don't care about the sun. I want to see my grandson play. It's a big day for him, and

I want to be there."

I stepped in to explain. "Dadi, we're worried about your health. The sun will be intense, and it's not safe for you to sit out there for hours. It could be very hard on you."

Still determined, Dadi insisted, "I'm not changing my mind. I want to be there for my Ved. You'll have to figure out a way to take me."

Realizing we couldn't change her mind, I finally agreed. "Alright, Dadi, we'll take you.

Later at the cricket ground, Dadi was carefully settled in a shaded area, ensuring her comfort while she cheered for Vedant.

Vedant's performance was nothing short of spectacular. He was outstanding and played with such class that it was impossible not to be impressed. Each stroke of the bat was executed with precision, and it was clear he was on fire. I couldn't help but think how brilliant it would have been if Mr. Sharma were there to witness this brilliance firsthand. Vedant was truly mind-blowing—until, of course, the most unexpected twist occurred. Just as he was approaching a well-deserved century, he got out at 99! It was a classic cricketing mishap that had us all groaning and chuckling. "So close, yet so far!" someone joked, and we all laughed despite the disappointment.

Despite this minor setback, we applauded Vedant's innings with genuine admiration. I had convinced myself that this would definitely not be his last inning; his talent was undeniable. But as the match progressed, fate seemed to have other plans for him.

His team, despite his heroic efforts, ended up losing the match. It felt like a cruel twist of fate—his stellar performance overshadowed by yet another defeat. And just when we thought things couldn't get worse, the wicketkeeper from the opposing team decided to steal the limelight. Agamjot Singh from the other side put on a show of his own, chasing down a monstrous total of 281 all by himself with an unbeaten 173.

It was the kind of performance that made you question whether you were watching a cricket match or a highlight reel of superhuman feats. As Agamjot Singh strutted around the field, it felt like he was giving a masterclass on how to single-handedly win a game. Meanwhile, Vedant's team could only watch in disbelief as their dreams slipped away.

I had assumed Vedant would be the saddest person on the field after such a crushing blow, but then I saw him chatting with Agamjot Singh. It seemed like he was soaking in every word from his opponent, trying to glean some wisdom from the extraordinary performance Agamjot had just delivered. It was a sight that perfectly captured the essence of sportsmanship.

Just a day ago, Vedant had been lamenting that this might be his last inning, and here he was, engaging with the player who had almost turned his innings into the final chapter of a fairytale. It was almost poetic—how life on the cricket field could take you from the depths of disappointment to a moment of learning and camaraderie. The important thing is the ultimate reaction to failure or a success.

I couldn't help but laugh at the irony of it all. The same player who had narrowly missed out on a century and faced a team loss was now laughing with the hero of the match. It was as if the sport had a way of turning its setbacks into opportunities for growth. "Haha, that's sports for you," I mused, appreciating the way cricket had once again shown its unpredictable and humbling nature.

"I'm so proud of my grandson," said Dadi.

When Dadi, Vedant, and I returned from the match, Dadi was bubbling with excitement to praise Vedant. As we walked in, we saw Mr. Shukla seated comfortably, enjoying a cup of tea made by Rima Aunty. Vedant's father, Santosh, was also there.

Dadi, eager to share her admiration, said, "Santosh, my Vedant plays like Gambhir!" Her face lit up with pride.

I added, "Dadi, Vedant's favorite player is Dhoni, just like Dhoni himself."

Dadi chuckled, "Well, since Vedant is a lefty, he's more like Gambhir." She laughed, "I know more about cricket than you think!"

Mr. Shukla, looking up from his tea, asked, "Who won the match?"

Vedant muttered, "We lost."

Mr. Sharma grinned, "Hmm, I see."

Dadi, undeterred, exclaimed, "But Vedant scored 99 runs!" "Nice, Vedant!" Mr. Shukla complimented, raising his cup. "Still lost?" Mr. Sharma inquired, puzzled. "Why?"

Vedant replied, "The opposing team's batsman played exceptionally well."

Mr. Sharma shook his head and remarked, "I always say— sports are a waste of time. Ridiculous."

As the conversation continued, Vedant's frustration was palpable. His disappointment was not just about the match, but also the lack of understanding and support from those around him. He felt the sting of his near-miss, the weight of unfulfilled expectations, and the sting of his father's dismissive attitude.

Days later, It was a Sunday morning at Vedant's house, and the atmosphere was thick with anticipation. Dr. Sharma's attention focused on a large batch of jalebis placing at the dining table. The sweet aroma of the fried treats wafted through the house, mixing with the usual Sunday morning bustle. Rima Aunty, as always, was busy with her kitchen chores. Radhika Didi had gone out for her campaign. Dadi, Vedant, and I were huddled together, waiting anxiously for the newspaper to arrive. As the selection result is come out in a newspaper this time.

Every few minutes, Ved glance towards the door, hoping to see the newspaper boy's arrival. The normally bustling house felt unusually quiet, punctuated only by the occasional sizzle of the jalebis and Rima Aunty's soft murmurs as she worked in the kitchen.

As the minutes ticked by, Dadi broke the silence. "When will that newspaper arrive?" she murmured, her voice tinged with worry.

Just then, the newspaper boy sailed the paper through the open balcony like an aeroplane while he continued pedaling his bicycle down the street. Vedant sprang up with a burst of energy, catching the newspaper mid-air as it landed neatly in the hall.

With a deep breath, Vedant unfolded the newspaper. The moment felt like it was stretching out endlessly. Dadi and I leaned in, our eyes glued to the page, hoping for the best but fearing the worst.

Vedant's fingers trembled as he scanned the list. The seconds felt like hours. Finally, his eyes stopped, and his shoulders slumped. The name he was searching for was not there.

Dr. Sharma, wiping his hands on a towel, noticing the somber atmosphere.

"What happened?" he asked.

Vedant looked up, his face a picture of disappointment. "I didn't make it again," he said quietly.

Dr. Sharma's face softened slightly, but he quickly masked his empathy with a nonchalant tone. "Well, better luck next time. You can always focus on other things."

Just then, Dadi's eyes lit up as she squinted at the newspaper. "Ved, look! Your name is here!" she said, her voice trembling with excitement.

Vedant froze in place, unsure of what she meant. Slowly, he leaned over to see where she was pointing. At the corner of *the page, in a small box, it was written: "Vedant Sharma, the star wicketkeeper of Gomtinagar, gave his best for his team but didn't secure a spot in the U-19 state team. However, he has earned a place in the East Zone team of Uttar Pradesh."*

For a moment, Vedant was stuck in place, staring at the words as if he couldn't believe what he was seeing. His dream of the U-19 state team hadn't come true, but this was still something – something big. He had made it to the East Zone team. Slowly, the realization sank in, but he didn't know how to react. He stood there, silent, as the words replayed in his mind.

I could feel the excitement bubbling inside me. I couldn't contain it anymore and grabbed Vedant by the shoulders, trying to lift him as if my energy could snap him out of his shock. "Ved! You made it! You're in the East Zone team! This is huge!" I shouted, grinning from ear to ear.

Vedant blinked, as if waking up from a dream, and a small smile finally started to spread across his face. Dadi, unable to contain her pride, beamed at her grandson. "I told you, my Ved plays like Gambhir! He never gives up," she said, her voice full of love and admiration.

Just a second after Dadi had announced Vedant's selection, Mr. Sharma snatched the newspaper from her hands and scanned the small box where his son's name was written. His eyes narrowed as he read the words carefully, the lines on his forehead softening into a calm expression. He finished reading and turned to Vedant, his stern voice cutting through the excitement.

"When will the matches for the East Zone happen?" he asked, his tone more serious than celebratory.

Vedant, still in a mild state of disbelief, managed to reply, "After a month."

There was a pause, a moment of silence that felt heavier than it needed to be. Mr. Sharma looked at his son for a few seconds longer, and then, to everyone's surprise, a small, cheeky smile crept onto his face. He straightened the newspaper in his hands and spoke in a way that almost seemed out of character.

"We'll all come to watch," he said, nodding slightly as if he was giving his approval to something he had long been skeptical of. His smile remained subtle but warm, a rare moment of support shining through his usually reserved demeanor.

Vedant's eyes lit up with joy. It was as if all the tension, disappointment, and uncertainty of the last few weeks had evaporated in that instant. I saw the glitter in his eyes, the spark that had been missing since the results came out. He stood a little taller, his shoulders no longer weighed down by doubt.

Dadi, still beaming with pride, clapped her hands together softly. *"Santosh, dekho, finally tumhara beta apne dum pe kuchh kar dikhaya!"* she said, the twinkle in her eyes as bright as Vedant's.

Mr. Sharma raised an eyebrow but didn't say much. He was a man of few words when it came to matters of sports, always believing that academics should take precedence. But for today, for this moment, even he couldn't deny the pride he felt for his son.

I was about to make another light-hearted comment when the front door opened, and Radhika Didi stepped in. Her entry seemed to change the atmosphere instantly. While we were celebrating, her face looked troubled, worry lines creasing her forehead. Her usually radiant smile was nowhere to be found.

Vedant, still riding high on the moment, didn't notice her expression right away. "Didi!" I called out, grinning from ear to ear. "Ved made it into the East Zone!"

"Nice," she said, trying to force a smile, but it faltered almost immediately. "Congrats, Bhai," she added, her voice lacking its usual warmth.

Vedant, always quick to notice when something was off with his sister, turned toward her. His smile dimmed slightly, concern creeping into his features. "What's wrong, Didi? You don't look good. Is everything okay?"

Radhika sighed deeply, shaking her head. She seemed hesitant, like she wasn't sure whether she should say what was on her mind. But then, without warning, her frustration boiled over. "Nothing," she started, her voice tight with anger, "Just... *I swear, if I had a gun today, I would've killed him.*"

The room went silent. Dadi and I exchanged a glance, while Rima Aunty, who had been in the kitchen, came out to see what was going on.

Vedant took a step toward his sister, his excitement momentarily forgotten. "Who are you talking about? What happened?"

CHAPTER TWELVE

WAR OF FAITH

Radhika Didi clenched her fists, her body stiffening as she exhaled sharply. "That jerk, Vikki!" she hissed, her voice trembling with a mix of anger and frustration.

Ved's eyes widened with concern. "What did he do, Didi?"

"He started his own political rally, right against my campaign!" she snapped. "He's such a wreck of a person."

Radhika Didi's face tightened with frustration as she explained the situation to us. "Vikki has launched his own rally, promoting the idea that 'Communism is welfare,' and honestly, I don't completely disagree with that. I accept that communism can work in certain ways to support people. But my campaign is focused on something different. *I believe in individual freedom, the right of each person to make their own choices. That's what liberalism stands for*, and that's what I'm trying to promote. But Vikki, being the way he is, is using his brother's influence to take all the power. He's deliberately trying to overshadow my campaign and stop me from reaching people. It's so frustrating!"

"What's the problem with this boy? Always getting involved where he's not needed!" I muttered.

"Forget all this nonsense; these petty issues will keep coming up," Rima Aunty said as she brought in a large plate filled with Khaja from the kitchen. "Today is a special day for my dearest Ved. Let's celebrate!" she added, her face beaming with pride.

Khaja, a popular sweet from Bihar and Eastern UP, is a delicacy known for its crispiness and rich flavor. It's a traditional treat that's often enjoyed during special occasions.

"It came from Amma's house last week," Rima Aunty said, pointing towards Dadi with a smile.

We all sat down to enjoy the delicious Khaja from Kashi. Radhika Didi then turned to her father and asked, *"What do you think, Papa? Will India ever be truly independent?"*

"India is already independent, my daughter." The voice came from the doorway. My dad, stepping into the Sharma household, responded with a reassuring smile.

Rima Aunty greeted my dad with warmth as he entered the hall, her face lighting up with genuine hospitality. She moved gracefully towards him, and said, "Welcome, Bhai Sahab." Without missing a beat, she arranged a comfortable spot for him at the table, making sure he had the best seat. As she placed a plate of freshly arranged Khaja in front of him, she smiled and added, "Please, enjoy this special treat. It's from Amma's house in Kashi, brought just for occasions like this."

"occasion?" my dad asked.

"Ved has been selected for the East Zone team, Dad," I said.

"Very, very congratulations, Vedant," Dad said, his voice filled with pride.

Ved nodded with a smile, clearly pleased.

Just then, Radhika Didi interrupted with a concerned look and said, *"How is it independent, Uncle? I don't think so." She added.*

"Why don't you think so?" Dad asked.

"Because we don't have freedom of thought," Radhika Didi began passionately. *"We're just being controlled—by the system, by politics, by religion, by the expectations of society. We're not truly independent; we're trapped. True independence is the freedom of thought, just like liberty. But the thoughts we're allowed to think are actually part of the system's maze, and in that, we're losing our own identity,"* she added, her voice filled with frustration and conviction.

"What do you mean by 'own identity,' Radhika?" Dad asked, his tone calm but curious, trying to understand her deeper point.

"I just know, Uncle, that a *meaningful life gives you your true identity,"* Radhika Didi replied thoughtfully. *"Freedom of thought provides individual independence, and that's what liberalism is all about. It's through that personal independence that we can find our own autonomy and, ultimately, our identity."*

"What a brilliant mind you've given her, Bhabhi," Dad said, glancing at Rima Aunty with admiration. His eyes gleamed with pride as he acknowledged Radhika didi's sharp intellect.

"I don't think this sharp mind comes from Doctor Sahab; it must have come from you," Dad said, chuckling as he appreciated Radhika Didi's views. His lighthearted comment carried both humor and admiration, acknowledging the wisdom passed down from her mother.

"I appreciate your thoughts, beta," Dad said with a nod. "But tell me this—society's welfare is the ultimate goal, and for that, collective thinking is more important than individual thinking, isn't it?" He leaned forward, curious to hear her perspective, balancing between individual freedom and the needs of the greater community.

"Yes, Uncle," she replied thoughtfully, "but I believe that *collective individual thinking is the great way of societal welfare.*"

"Collective individual thinking!! ... Brilliant. You're amazing, Radhika!" Dad exclaimed, clearly impressed by her insight. His admiration was evident as he marveled at the depth of her thought, his face lighting up with pride.

She nodded with a smile, clearly pleased with Dad's praise.

Meanwhile, the rest of us had turned into silent spectators, like an audience at a debate, except our focus was less on philosophy and more on the delicious Khaja in front of us. We exchanged glances, silently agreeing that Radhika Didi could keep impressing Dad while we happily kept munching away!

"Vikki's approach is so narrow-minded," Radhika Didi said, frustration evident in her voice. "It's maddening how he uses his influence to push his own agenda. With the voting next month, he's worried that my campaign will cut into his brother's votes. He's even twisting my Liberty campaign into a protest against the constitution, which is causing friction within specific communities. How do I get that fool to understand?" she added, shaking her head in exasperation.

"I'll explain it to him tomorrow—with my bat," Ved said.

"No, there's no need for you to explain anything," Rima Aunty said firmly, cutting him off before he could even think about it.

"Look, he's an ignorant fool and the brother of an MLA. It's better not to get involved with him," Mr. Sharma advised, his tone cautious and firm.

"But Papa, he's interfering with my work, and I won't let it go. If he tries something again, I won't stay quiet," Radhika Didi said, her voice full of determination.

"Look, beta, spreading awareness and motivating society is good, but you don't necessarily need a campaign to do that," Dad said thoughtfully. *"Change yourself, and society will change on its own.* That's what Mahatma Gandhi believed. By becoming independent yourself and escaping the matrix, you can give people a vision to follow. Remember, actions speak louder than words."

"Thank you, Uncle, I'll remember your words," Radhika Didi said, her expression softening as she absorbed the wisdom in his advice.

"Didi, if he tries to say something again, let me know," Ved said, his tone earnest and protective.

"Better if you play your game," Didi replied with a smile, encouraging Ved to stay on track with his own pursuits.

"When is your first match for the zone?" I asked Ved.

"Next month, on the first Monday. It's in Basti district, near Ayodhya," Vedant replied.

"Shit!! I can't come to watch," I said, frustrated. "I have to leave for Jodhpur at the end of this month."

"No worries," Ved said with a mischievous grin, "but you're going to miss witnessing a classic century. Bad luck!" His tone was light and teasing, making the best of the situation.

Finally, after so many attempts, Ved got selected somewhere, I thought to myself. I hope this is just the beginning for him.

The next day, Ved came to my house to invite me to go to Radhika Didi's campaign. I asked him, "Did she call us?"

"No," he replied, "but I want to go and confront Vikki. I've got a plan to take him down. Are you coming or not?"

Reluctantly, I had to agree and say yes.

As we reached the place, the scene was nothing short of chaotic. The air was thick with tension and the roar of the crowd. It felt as if the entire area was caught in the throes of a massive riot.

"What's happening?" I shouted as I urged Ved to stop the scooty

"Looks like there's been some kind of riot," Ved said.

We saw people fighting with each other everywhere. "Where is Radhika Di?" Ved asked, his voice filled with urgency and concern.

"I don't know," I replied.

"She said the campaign was happening at Govind Maidan, but all I see here is fighting. And where's the police?" Ved said.

"Call your father," I suggested.

"What can he do?" Ved said, shaking his head. "We need to find Didi first."

"Jai Shree Ram..." A loud group shouted from behind us, their voices booming. They were all carrying orange flags.

"Ved, let's move this way," I said urgently. We hurried down a narrow street to hide from them.

"Didi, where are you?" Ved shouted into the commotion. "I'll call her," I said, reaching for my phone.

Just then, a voice came from behind us. "What are you two doing here?"

"Oh, thank God, you're okay," Ved said, relieved to see Radhika Didi.

"What are you doing here? The situation isn't safe," Radhika Didi said. "The city is in trouble now."

"What happened?" I asked, trying to make sense of the chaos.

"Vikki's brother, Seenu, has been murdered," Radhika Didi said.

"What??" I was shocked.

"How?" Ved asked, trying to grasp the situation.

"Someone killed him," Radhika Didi explained. "And the local members of Seenu's party believe Sahil did it."

"Sahil?" I asked, confused.

"He's the leader of the opposing party," Didi clarified.

"Then why is all this happening?" I asked, trying to understand the chaos.

"Because Vikki wants revenge. He openly declared in the media that he will kill Sahil himself," Didi said.

"Has the police taken any action?" I inquired. "Not yet," she replied.

"Seenu's party is aligned with Hindu ideologies and most of its members are Hindu, while Sahil's party follows Islamic ideology and consists mostly of Muslims. After Seenu's death, "Vikki publicly made aggressive statements about the Muslim ideology, which ignited clashes between the two groups," Radhika Didi explained.

We were hiding when we saw a man with a green flag shoot another man who was holding a saffron flag.

We were terrified. We needed to get home quickly and stay away from all this chaos.

"We'll have to stay here until things calm down," Radhika Didi said. "I've called the police. They should be arriving soon."

We were hiding in the alley when we saw crowds approaching from both sides.

"We can't stay here much longer," Ved said anxiously. "Yeah, but we can't go out either," I replied.

"I'll try to make it to the scooty outside," Ved suggested. "Once I'm there, you both follow. We need to get out of here quickly before things get worse," he added, his voice tense.

"No, you're not going anywhere!" Radhika Didi said firmly.

"We don't have any other choice," Ved replied, his determination clear. "Wait here, both of you," he added, stepping cautiously toward the exit of the alley.

Just as Ved was about to reach the scooty, someone hurled a stone at him.

"Ved!" We screamed in panic.

"Kill the Kafir! Kill him!" The shouts grew louder, coming closer to us.

"Run, get out of here!" Ved yelled, sprinting back toward us. Without a second thought, we turned and dashed in the opposite direction of the alley

We sprinted as fast as we could and finally reached a nearby school. Panting heavily, we quickly scanned the area.

"Let's hide here for a while," I suggested, looking around for a safe spot.

We hurried towards the gate, hoping the walls of the school would give us some shelter from the chaos outside.

As we huddled in the shadow of the school, the sounds of distant chaos echoed in the air. It was unsettling, yet the quiet of the school grounds offered a momentary pause from the turmoil outside. We caught our breath, and I finally broke the silence.

"How did this all escalate so fast?" I asked, still shaken. "Why would Sahil kill Seenu? It doesn't make any sense."

Radhika Didi, leaning against the wall, shook her head. "I don't know the full details, honestly. It's all so tangled in political affairs. The exact truth is hard to figure out, especially when the media and parties start spinning their own narratives."

"But what about your campaign? Is it somehow connected to this mess?" I asked, my concern growing for her.

"No, it has nothing to do with my campaign," Didi said firmly, brushing off the notion. "This is a communal riot, plain and simple. It's the kind of thing that keeps happening in India, over and over again. And people like us —get caught in the middle. Our thoughts, our lives, everything we work for, gets crushed under the weight of these conflicts."

"We need to go. Now," Ved whispered urgently. "Where? They're everywhere!" I muttered, panic rising.

"Stay low! Don't let them see us," Radhika Didi said, her voice barely above a whisper.

"Kill the Kafirs! Kill them all!" the mob's voices shouted, getting louder.

"They're coming this way!" Ved hissed, his eyes darting around.

"We can't stay here," Radhika Didi replied, glancing around for an escape.

"They've spotted us! Ved, they're coming!" I stammered, my heart racing.

"Run!" Ved grabbed my arm and pulled me forward.

"Don't stop, don't look back!" Radhika Didi urged, pulling me along too.

"There they are! They're hiding!" a voice shouted from behind us.

"Faster! They're gaining!" Ved gasped.

"I can't! My legs—" I choked out, struggling to keep pace. "You have to! Move!" Radhika Didi ordered.

A stone crashed nearby, startling us. "That was close!" I said, out of breath.

Ved pointed ahead, "In there, the window! Go!" We scrambled inside, hearts pounding.

"Are they... gone?" I whispered, barely able to catch my breath.

"Shhh! They're still looking," Ved replied, peeking out cautiously.

"Stay quiet. Don't make a sound," Radhika Didi warned, crouching lower.

"Kill the Bastards! Find them!" the mob's voice roared, closer now.

"We're trapped," I muttered, trembling.

"Run faster!" Ved urged as we sprinted through the narrow streets.

We reached Hanuman Chowk, breathless, the chaos still echoing behind us.

"Almost there," I muttered, glancing back.

We turned into Amir's street, only to freeze in our tracks. "Stop!" Radhika Didi whispered sharply.

Vikki stood there, right in front of us, surrounded by his thugs. Guns, sticks, and carpenter's tools glinted in their hands.

The bald, towering thug—at least six feet tall and broad— stepped forward, raising his gun. The cold metal pointed straight at us.

"Stop," Vikki ordered, stepping forward.

"They're all Hindus. Let them go," he added, signaling to his men.

Ved clenched his fists, glaring at Vikki. "You think that makes this okay?"

Radhika Didi squeezed Ved's arm, whispering, "Not now."

"I'll deal with you later," Vikki said, glaring at Radhika Didi.

Vikki and his men turned and walked away, their voices echoing through the street.

"Jai Shree Ram!" they shouted, their chants fading into the distance.

As we caught our breath and the chaos of Vikki's departure began to settle, we heard the distant shouts of another group approaching. Our relief was short-lived as a new wave of fear washed over us.

"Quick, find somewhere to hide!" Ved urged, pulling us into the shadows of an abandoned building.

We barely had time to catch our breath before the sounds of footsteps and aggressive voices filled the air. Sahil's thugs had arrived, their aggressive mannerisms and angry shouts unmistakable.

"Stay quiet," I whispered.

Suddenly, the thugs burst into the alley, their leader, a burly man with a scar running down his face, at the forefront.

"Search every corner!" he barked.

We exchanged anxious glances as the thugs started to fan out, their flashlights probing the darkness. Radhika Didi's face went pale, her hand gripping mine tightly.

"We shouldn't have come here," I muttered. "Finding a way out is crucial now," Ved said.

"Police!" Ved suddenly shouted, pointing toward a distant figure in uniform. "Let's get to them!"

We nodded in agreement.

We sprinted toward the police officers, our hearts racing as we closed the distance. But our relief was short-lived when we saw one of the policemen collapse, a dark red stain spreading across his uniform.

The burly man, a menacing grin on his face, held a smoking gun. He had fired a shot that felled the policeman. Panic surged through us.

"Sir, save us!" Ved shouted, as we were just 50 meters away from the police.

Just then, the burly man turned toward us. His grin widened as he raised his gun and aimed directly at us.

"Run, run, run!" Ved urged.

As we turned to flee, the burly man's shot rang out behind us.

CHAPTER THIRTEEN

END OF A DREAM

"Ved! Ved!" I screamed, as I rushed toward him. *"Bhai!" Radhika Didi shouted,* her face pale with fear.

We ran to Vedant, his body crumpled on the street, blood pooling around him. The burly man who had shot him was tackled by the police, but none of that mattered now. All I could see was Ved, lying motionless.

"Sir, please help us!" I shouted desperately to the officers.

"Please, do something!" Radhika Didi cried, her hands trembling as she cradled Ved's head in her lap, tears streaming down her cheeks.

"Get him to the hospital, now!" the sergeant ordered.

The officers quickly lifted Ved into the police Jeep. The engine roared to life, cutting through the chaos of the riot.

"We have to move, fast!" one officer shouted, his hands covered in Ved's blood as he helped load him into the vehicle.

I fumbled for my phone, hands shaking. "Aunty... it's Ved... he's been shot. We're on our way to the hospital. Hurry!" My voice broke as I tried to stay calm, but the panic surged.

No response. Just static.

"Aunty! Ved..." I repeated, breathless.

Finally, a voice came through, faint but urgent. "Where are you? What happened?" said Rima Aunty.

"Aunty, Ved's been shot! We're rushing him to the hospital!" I blurted out, feeling my heart pound in my chest.

The Jeep sped through the streets, sirens blaring. Radhika Didi clutched Ved's hand tightly, whispering, "Hold on, Ved. Just hold on... we're almost there."

"Make way, make way!" one of the officers shouted as we arrived at the hospital. The police Jeep screeched to a halt in front of the emergency entrance.

"Get a stretcher! Now!" the sergeant barked at the hospital staff.

Two nurses rushed out, quickly pulling a stretcher towards us. Vedant lay still in the back, his shirt soaked with blood. Radhika Didi and I scrambled out of the Jeep, our hearts racing.

The nurses rolled him inside as fast as they could, and we followed close behind.

"Doctor! Gunshot wound, he's losing a lot of blood!" a nurse called out.

A team of doctors rushed to Ved's side, quickly moving him into a nearby room. I tried to follow, but a nurse stopped us. "You can't go any further. Let us handle it."

I stood there, frozen, not knowing what to do.

Just then, my phone buzzed. It was my dad. I answered it quickly.

"We're almost there. Where's Ved?" Dad asked, his voice tense.

"We're at the emergency room. The doctors just took him in. I don't know what's happening yet..." I said.

Moments later, I saw Mr. Sharma, Rima Aunty, and Dadi rushing toward us. Rima Aunty's eyes were wide with fear, and Dadi was already in tears.

"Where is he? How's my boy?" Rima Aunty asked, gripping my arm tightly.

"He's inside. They're treating him now," I said, barely able to speak.

Rima Aunty collapsed into tears, and Dadi hugged her tightly.

We stood in silence, the hallway's cold sterility amplified by the heavy air thick with tension. Rima Aunty's sobs echoed, a piercing reminder of our anxiety, while the faint cries and beeping monitors from the emergency room punctuated the silence. A few others, similarly caught in the aftermath of the riots, had gathered around, their faces a mix of fear and desperation. Rima Aunty and Dadi wept quietly, while Radhika Didi sat motionless, her eyes fixed intently on the door of the operating room, awaiting any sign of news.

Mr. Sharma, with his arms crossed, stared at the ground, while my dad sat on the bench, his hands resting on his knees. A man in his mid-forties, dressed in simple clothes, approached Mr. Sharma. He had a bandage wrapped around his arm. "Another one caught in the middle of this madness?" the man asked quietly, nodding toward the room where Ved was being treated.

"Mine's inside too," the man said, his voice bitter. "This riot, this whole thing... what's it for? I don't even know who started it. They've torn apart families, businesses, everything."

Another older man, who was sitting nearby, chimed in. "It's all politics. They fuel this nonsense for their own gains. We, the common people, are just pawns to them. It's the poor and the middle class who bleed." His tone was weary, as if he'd seen it too many times before.

The man with the bandage shook his head bitterly. "You're right. We bust our backs trying to live a decent life, and then one riot, one clash, and everything crumbles. They're safe in their mansions, we're the ones left picking up the pieces."

Mr. Sharma, standing tall, looked at the man. "It's always the same. People in power make these speeches, fuel the fire, and the common man pays the price. My Ved is barely 19, and now he's in there because some fools couldn't control their hatred."

Another man, maybe in his late forties, piped up, his voice dripping with frustration. "The middle class always gets the worst of it. We're the ones who take the hits, lose our businesses, our kids. We aren't rich enough to escape, not poor enough to be invisible. We're stuck in the middle, paying the price for every riot, every hike in taxes, every economic downturn."

Mr. Sharma's voice was filled with frustration. "I tried to keep Ved away from all of this. Focus on studies, do something productive. But how can we keep them safe when the whole society is burning around them?"

"Education was supposed to be our way out," Dad said quietly. "But even education doesn't save you from bullets. A degree can't shield you from hate."

The hopelessness in the room was thick, the shared frustration palpable. We were strangers in that moment, but connected by the same suffocating reality. We waited in silence, hoping for a miracle as the door to the operation room stayed firmly shut.

Suddenly, the door to the emergency room opened, and a doctor stepped out, his face grim.

Everyone fell silent. Our hearts stopped. "Vedant Sharma's family?" he asked.

We all stood, fear clenching in our chests.

"The next few hours are critical," the doctor said, his voice flat. "We're doing everything we can."

Rima Aunty collapsed back onto the bench, tears streaming down her face once again. Dadi closed her eyes, whispering prayers under her breath, perhaps seeking solace from Shiv Ji. Mr. Sharma gripped the edge of the bench so tightly that his knuckles turned white.

Hours passed, each second heavier than the last. I stood by the door, staring down the hallway, praying the doctor would emerge with good news. But deep down, I knew the truth. I could feel it in the weight that hung over all of us, suffocating.

Mr. Sharma was pacing restlessly, muttering under his breath. "This country... this system," he said, shaking his head. "How many more children have to die before someone does something? Every day, riots... Every day, politics."

My father, quiet for most of the time, looked at the man and said, "It's not just about being common. Even those with money, with power, are helpless in moments like these. When violence breaks out, it doesn't ask about your wealth or status."

Another older man, whose niece had been injured, leaned forward. "What's worse is that it's all orchestrated. These leaders pit us against each other, all for votes and power. And who pays the price? Innocent lives."

The doors to the emergency room suddenly swung open, and the doctor emerged, his face grim. The conversation died instantly as all eyes turned toward him.

He didn't need to say a word. His expression told us everything.

"I'm sorry," he finally whispered. "We did everything we could."

The world seemed to stop. Rima Aunty let out a wail that echoed through the sterile hospital corridors, her body crumpling with grief. Dadi, still clutching her prayer beads, let them slip from her hands as tears streamed silently down her wrinkled face. Mr. Sharma fell back into the bench, shaking his head in disbelief.

I couldn't move. The sound of my heart thudded in my ears, drowning out everything. Ved... was gone.

The hospital was left behind in a fog of disbelief. Vedant's lifeless body was carried out, wrapped in white, but no one seemed able to comprehend that it was him. His face, once full of dreams and mischief, was now as still as stone.

The air was heavy with silence, broken only by the faint sound of sobbing from Rima Aunty and Dadi, their hearts shattered beyond repair.

Mr. Sharma stood in the corner, his eyes red, his body rigid, trying to maintain some composure. I couldn't bear to look at them for long. My own legs felt weak, and the weight of the moment pressed down like a boulder.

The police helped carry Vedant's body out of the hospital, wrapping him gently, almost too gently, as though they feared he might break. Outside, a police jeep waited, and the streets—usually alive with noise—had fallen into an eerie stillness.

The drive back home was unbearable. As we arrived, a crowd had already gathered. Mr. Shukla from next door, Gauri Aunty with her son Pranjal, and several other neighbors and relatives stood at the gate. They wore expressions of disbelief and sorrow.

Mr. Shukla from next door approached first, his face grim. "I can't believe this," he said, shaking his head. "Riots took him? Such a young boy, what sense is there in this madness?"

Beside him, Gauri Aunty, Mr. Sharma's sister, wiped her tears. "How many more families have to go through this? Our children... taken by mindless violence."

My father, standing with us, finally broke his silence, his voice rough with emotion. "It's a broken system. Politicians use these riots for their own gains, and families like ours are left to pick up the pieces."

Rima Aunty and Dadi sat beside Vedant's body, their sobs gut-wrenching, while Mr. Sharma knelt beside them, his head bowed in silent prayer. I couldn't move. My throat tightened as I watched Radhika Didi hold Ved's cold hand, her tears falling silently onto his shroud.

The mourners sat around in small groups, some in shock, others quietly talking.

Pandit Ji arrived, and the final rites began. Vedant was gently prepared for his last journey, adorned with marigolds and sandalwood.

The procession to Baikunth Dham began at dusk. Vedant's body was placed on a bamboo stretcher, carried on the

shoulders of his father, me, and a few other men. As we moved slowly, the air filled with the steady chant of "Ram naam satya hai." The words echoed through the quiet streets, mingling with the muffled sobs of the crowd.

Finally, we reached Baikunth Dham. The pyre was ready, and Pandit Ji began the rituals. Vedant's body, draped in white and adorned with garlands of marigolds, was gently placed on the wooden pyre. The scent of sandalwood and camphor lingered as Pandit Ji began the rituals, his voice steady despite the palpable sadness around us.

"The body is anointed with ghee," Pandit Ji explained softly, as he smeared the clarified butter across Ved's forehead, symbolizing purity in the final journey. He handed small pouches of sandalwood and mango leaves to Mr. Sharma and my father. Together, they carefully placed them onto the pyre, mixing with the corkwood that had been arranged as the base.

The air was thick with incense, mingling with the natural scent of the earth and river, creating an atmosphere both peaceful and agonizing.

The crowd was silent, but the tension was palpable. Mr. Shukla stood beside us, his face grim. "This is what we have left," he muttered, "rituals to honor the dead while the living are left in chaos."

As Pandit Ji chanted the sacred mantras, Mr. Sharma lit the flame, his face stoic, though his eyes betrayed the storm inside him. I watched as the fire consumed the wood, the smoke rising toward the darkening sky, carrying with it the soul of my best friend.

Tears blurred my vision, and as I watched the flames rise, a deep emptiness settled into my heart. The finality of it all hit me—the loss, the unfairness, the unanswered questions. All I could hear were the faint murmurs of grief and frustration around me, as if the fire was consuming not just Ved, but the hope we once had for our future.

Emotions had enveloped us in a heavy silence following Vedant's funeral. For days, everything felt eerily quiet, as if the world had paused to mourn. It was a time of reflection and sorrow, where the weight of loss hung heavily over us.

About ten days later, as I prepared to leave for Jodhpur for my Engineering studies at IIT Jodhpur, the atmosphere was still thick with the remnants of grief. Packing my bag, I came across an old camouflage cap tucked away in the corner of my drawer. It was the one Vedant had given me, with his autograph scrawled across it.

I remembered his words vividly: "When I play for India, you might have to wait in a long line or even jump onto the field just to get my autograph, like people do for Dhoni. So, I'm signing it now. Keep it; it will be worth something someday."

At the time, I had laughed at his playful bravado, imagining a future where Vedant would be a celebrated cricketer. But now, as I held the cap in my hands, the laughter was replaced by a teary smile. The cap had become a symbol of his dreams, and though he was no longer with us, his spirit and aspirations lived on in that simple, cherished memento.

As I approached the Sharma house, a heavy silence hung in the air. The usually lively home felt eerily still. I walked onto the balcony, taking in the quietness that surrounded the place. No one seemed to be around. I went inside, heading toward Mr. Sharma's clinic room where he would always be, but it was empty.

Puzzled, I made my way to the kitchen, expecting to see Rima Aunty busy with something, but she wasn't there either. The whole house felt deserted. I figured they must have gone out. Just as I was about to leave, I heard a familiar voice behind me.

"Oh, hey! Looks like you're heading off to Jodhpur,"

Radhika Didi called from the hallway.

I turned around, surprised. "Ah, yes," I replied, offering a small smile.

"Where is everyone? It's so quiet here," I asked, still wondering about the empty house.

She stepped closer, her expression softening. "Dadi's sleeping, and Papa took Mom to the orphanage to serve food in Ved's name," she explained quietly.

I nodded, the weight of her words sinking in. "When are you leaving?" she asked.

"I was just about to head out," I said, adjusting my bag.

"Okay then. All the best for your future. Have a great life, Mr. IITian," she said with a warm smile, a hint of pride in her voice.

I chuckled softly, "Thanks, Didi. Say my goodbye to everyone for me.

She nodded.

As I left the Sharma house and headed home, I felt the weight of everything sinking in. The silence, the goodbyes. When I reached home, Dad was already waiting for me by the gate, leaning casually against the wall, his arms crossed, wearing that familiar, unreadable expression.

"You ready, or still pretending to pack at the last minute?" he asked with a grin.

"All packed," I replied.

"Good." He gave me a light pat on the shoulder. "But remember, no matter where you go, you're still you. Don't forget that."

We stood there for a moment, the air heavy despite the lighthearted banter. Dad's expression turned a bit more serious. "Stay grounded, okay? Life will throw challenges at you, but a sense of humor will help you get through it."

"I got it, Dad," I nodded.

As I entered the car, Dad smiled and said,

Connect with your craft and discover your true identity. Enjoy the Mechanics Champ!

And just then, my phone rang. "Ananya!" I answered.

"Hiieee!" she said, her excitement palpable. "Where are you? When will you be here?"

"I'll reach by tomorrow morning," I replied. "Great, I'll see you at the gate then," she said.

As I arrived in Jodhpur that morning, the city greeted me with a unique charm. Although I was familiar with Rajasthan from my time in Kota, Jodhpur felt distinct. The sun was just rising, casting a golden hue over the city. The blue buildings of the old town, with their intricate carvings and latticework, created a stunning contrast against the arid landscape. The towering Mehrangarh Fort loomed majestically in the distance, its ancient walls bathed in the soft morning light.

The streets below were already alive with activity. I could see vendors setting up their stalls, offering an array of colorful spices, vibrant fabrics, and handcrafted jewelry. The aroma of freshly baked pyaaz ki kachoris and spicy mirchi vadas wafted through the air, mingling with the scent of incense and tea. Traditional Rajasthani folk music played softly, its rhythmic beats and melodious tunes adding to the city's vibrant atmosphere. The bustling markets, with their lively chatter and the clinking of bangles, created a sensory feast.

As I took in the sights and sounds, the warm, welcoming vibe of Jodhpur began to sink in. The city's rich cultural heritage was evident in every corner, from the ornate architecture to the delicious street food, making me feel both excited and at home as I prepared to start this new chapter.

As I reached the IIT gate, I spotted Ananya waiting. Her brown hair still fell like a cascading waterfall over her shoulders. When I approached, she greeted me with a warm hug and, with a playful grin, said, *"Welcome to the Indian Institute of Technology, Sir!"*

CHAPTER FOURTEEN

THE PRIDE

Two years later 15 June 2024,
Gomtinagar Station, Lucknow

The train screeched to a halt, and as Ananya and I stepped onto the platform, a wave of nostalgia washed over me. Everything looked the same, almost as if time had forgotten to move forward in this corner of the world.

We started walking towards the exit, and as we passed through the familiar streets, the memories came flooding back.

"Look, there's Ramu Bhaiya," I pointed to the corner stall, where the same man was making his signature jalebis, his hands moving with the precision of someone who had done it a thousand times.

Ananya chuckled. "I swear, he's been doing that since forever."

"And that dog," I added, watching the scruffy stray barking madly at the passersby. "Still claiming his territory."

As we continued, the old lady was there, crouched low, brooming the dusty street as if her only mission in life was to keep that small patch of road spotless.

"It's like a time capsule," I murmured, more to myself than to Ananya. "Nothing's changed."

When we reached the small Shiva temple, the buzz of activity remained unchanged. The familiar ringing of bells, the smell of incense, and the murmur of prayers filled the air.

"I used to walk past this every day," I said softly, feeling the pull of the past in every corner of the city.

Ananya glanced at me, "Do we heading home first?"

I hesitated, my eyes drifting down the road. That's when I saw it — *GCC. Golu Chaiwala Centre*. The small tea stall where Ved, Amir, and I had spent countless hours, sipping tea and talking about our dreams.

"Wait," I said, slowing down. "Let's stop at Golu Bhaiya's."

Ananya followed my gaze and smiled. "That's the famous GCC you used to talk about?"

I nodded, already feeling a bittersweet nostalgia. "Yeah... Ved, Amir, and I used to come here almost every evening. We called it 'special time with special tea.'"

As we approached the stall, Golu Bhaiya, the owner, looked up from his stove. His eyes lit up in recognition.

"Arre, Sangam bhaiya! Long time no see!" he called out with a grin, wiping his hands on his apron.

I smiled back. "Golu Bhaiya! Still serving the best chai in town?"

He laughed heartily. "Kya bhaiya, this chai isn't going anywhere! Special one for you today?"

"Of course," I replied, my heart warming at the familiarity. "Two specials, please."

As we sat on the small wooden bench outside, Golu Bhaiya served us the hot tea in little clay cups, the same way he always had. The rich aroma filled the air as I took a sip, instantly transported back to the days when Ved and I would sit here, laughing and dreaming.

"This is amazing," Ananya said, savoring the tea.

"Yeah," I replied, staring down at the cup, my mind flooded with memories. "Ved used to say Golu Bhaiya's chai could solve any problem. And honestly, some days it felt like it did."

With that, we continued our walk, and soon enough, the familiar sights of Gomtinagar reappeared.

"Before we go home... I want to stop by the Sharma house," I said quietly.

We crossed the street, and as we neared the house, the familiar fragrance of freshly made parathas hit me. "Rima Aunty," I whispered, smiling at the memory. "Still making her famous parathas."

Ananya gave me a sideways glance. "I think I can smell them from here."

I nodded, but my smile faltered as my gaze shifted toward the clinic. "And Dr. Sharma... always busy with patients."

The clinic looked just the same, filled with people waiting outside, chatting quietly. It was like nothing had changed.

We walked closer, and then I saw her — Dadi, sitting on the balcony, beads in hand, quietly chanting Shiva's name like she always did.

"Dadi's still here, still the same," I said quietly, feeling a lump form in my throat.

"You want to go in?" Ananya asked gently.

I shook my head, not quite ready. "Not yet. Let's just... stay here for a moment."

Suddenly, Rima Aunty emerged from the kitchen, her hands full with a plate of parathas. She set them on the dining table and, as she turned, her gaze fell on me standing in the balcony.

"Sangam!" she exclaimed with wide eyes, clearly surprised to see me after so long.

I smiled and waved. "Rima Aunty!"

She rushed to the balcony with an affectionate smile. "You've become such a stranger!" she chided playfully, wiping her hands on her apron. "You don't even visit anymore."

"I know, Aunty. It's been too long," I replied, feeling a little guilty. "But I'm here now."

Ananya and I walked to the hall, we both touched Dadi's feet. Dadi blessed us, her soft hands resting on my head. "Stay blessed, my child," she murmured, her voice as gentle as ever.

"Dadi, this is Ananya," I introduced her.

Ananya greeted them politely, and I introduced her to Rima Aunty too. Aunty's eyes sparkled with curiosity, but she smiled warmly.

"Come, come inside," Rima Aunty urged, leading us to the dining table. "I just made fresh parathas."

As we sat down, the smell of buttered parathas filled the air, making my stomach rumble with hunger. "I've missed this," I said, grabbing a plate with excitement.

Just as we started eating, Dr. Sharma walked in. "Sangam! What a surprise," he greeted me with a firm handshake. "I heard you were back."

"Just for a little while," I replied, feeling the warmth of being back in their home.

Dr. Sharma joined us at the table, and for a few moments, we ate in comfortable silence, enjoying Rima Aunty's homemade food. Then, I couldn't help but ask, "Where's Radhika didi? I didn't see her around."

Rima Aunty looked up from her plate, smiling softly. "She's at school, teaching. She's a teacher now, you know."

I raised my eyebrows in surprise. "Wow, that's amazing."

Before I could say anything more, the balcony door creaked open, and there she was—Radhika didi, walking in with an air of confidence. She was the only one who seemed to have changed. Her always-open hair was now tied in a neat bun, and her eyes had glasses, giving the full vibe of a proper teacher. A leather bag hung casually from her shoulder, swaying slightly as she walked.

But it wasn't just her. A young boy, no older than seven or eight, walked beside her, holding her hand. He looked up at her with admiration, his little steps quick to match her pace.

When Radhika didi saw me, her face lit up with a smile she couldn't contain. She walked toward me eagerly, her pace quickening as she closed the gap between us.

"Sangam!" she exclaimed, wrapping me in a warm hug. It felt like no time had passed.

I hugged her back, grinning from ear to ear. "Radhika didi! You look so different," I teased, looking her over. "You've become a proper teacher!"

She laughed, adjusting her glasses with a shy smile. "Well, time changes things, doesn't it?"

I gestured to Ananya. "This is Ananya. We've been traveling together."

Didi's smile widened as she shook Ananya's hand. "It's so nice to meet you."

Ananya smiled back. "I've heard so much about you."

"And who's this little one?" I asked, glancing at the boy standing beside Radhika didi.

Radhika didi smiled down at the boy, then looked back at me. "This is Raghav, my student... more like a brother now. He stays with me always. I took him from the orphanage last year."

Hearing that, I couldn't help but feel a wave of memories hit me—memories of Vedant. My expression must have changed because didi caught on right away.

She gently touched my arm and said softly, "You've taken on a lot of things today." Her eyes flicked toward the bags surrounding us. "Did you come straight here? Haven't you been home yet?"

I shook off the emotion with a faint smile. "Just heading there now. I'll see you later."

Later that night, as Dad, Ananya, and I sat down for dinner, I couldn't shake the feeling of emptiness. Vedant was gone forever, but I hadn't seen Amir since he left for Varanasi. The thought of my missing buddies weighed on me, and the quietness of the meal only deepened that feeling.

Unable to hold back, I looked up from my plate and asked, "Dad, How's Amir?"

Dad glanced at me with a slight smile, as if he had been waiting for the question. "Funny you ask," he said, setting down his fork. "He's coming at the end of the week. I told him you're here."

I felt a surge of excitement, but before I could respond, Dad continued, his tone more mysterious now. "And... there's a big surprise waiting for you. You're going to be shocked when you see the new Amir."

"New Amir?" I asked, eyebrows raised in amazement.

"Yup," Dad nodded, standing up from the table, leaving me hanging with curiosity. "You'll see soon enough."

As he left, I exchanged a glance with Ananya.

"Excited, huh?" she teased, noticing the anticipation on my face.

"Probably," I replied.

The end of the week arrived faster than I anticipated. The evening was cool, and a gentle breeze swept through the streets as I, along with Ananya and Dad, waited eagerly at the train station for Amir's arrival.

As the train pulled into the station, I scanned the crowd, hoping to catch a glimpse of Amir. Finally, I spotted him among the throngs of passengers. Amir was taller and leaner than I remembered, his presence commanding attention even from a distance. His face lit up with a broad smile as he spotted us.

"Amir!" I called out, waving enthusiastically.

He spotted me and grinned, quickening his pace. As he approached, we embraced warmly, and a wave of nostalgia swept over me.

"You look great!" I exclaimed, stepping back to take in his new appearance. Amir was sporting a fresh haircut and a more polished look, which made him look both distinguished and approachable.

"Thanks, Bhaiya," Amir replied, his eyes twinkling with excitement.

He then greeted Dad before I introduced Ananya to him with a playful nudge. "By the way, Amir, meet Ananya."

Ananya smiled and extended her hand. "Nice to meet you, Amir. I've heard quite a bit about you."

"The pleasure's mine," Amir said, shaking her hand. "I hope he hasn't bored you too much with his physics stories."

"Some were good ones," Ananya replied with a wink.

As we made our way to the station exit, Amir and I fell into easy conversation. The hustle and bustle of the station seemed to fade as we chatted.

"So, Dad mentioned something about a surprise," I said, trying to hide my curiosity. "You're looking all serious and proud. What's the scoop?"

Amir's face lit up with a mischievous grin. "Ah, the surprise. *I've been selected for the National Defence Academy (NDA).*"

I stopped in my tracks, my mouth slightly agape. "NDA? That's huge!"

"Yeah, well," Amir said, scratching his head with a sheepish grin, "it's a bit of a story. You see, my time in Kashi was eye-opening."

I raised an eyebrow. "Eye-opening? Do tell."

"I'll explain everything later," Amir said. "But I realized there's no greater honor than serving my country and living with pride. Everything else seemed secondary compared to that. That's why I prepared for the NDA, and here's the result."

I couldn't help but admire his transformation. "Man, you've changed so much in just two years. It's impressive."

Days later, the news about Amir joining the National Defence Academy (NDA) spread like wildfire through our neighborhood. It was remarkable to see how the dynamics had shifted. Neighbors who had once harshly criticized Amir's family now gathered with a newfound respect.

A group of men chatting at the local tea stall as we passed by them.

"Did you hear about Siddiqui's son?" one of them asked.

"Yes," another man responded. "He's joining the NDA! He's nothing like his father."

At the same time, another man chimed in, "You know, I always thought that boy was a troublemaker, but he's turned out to be quite the inspiration. Joining the NDA is no small feat."

"It's about time people recognized his worth," added another. "I've got nothing but respect for him now."

Amir, who overheard some of the conversations, was visibly pleased. He looked at me with a content smile. "I can die peacefully now," he said simply, reflecting the inner peace he had found in his new path.

The following week, our school organized a special program to honor Amir's achievement, as it was a proud moment for the school, too. The school grounds buzzed with excitement as Amir was introduced as a role model for the students. The principal, along with the staff, welcomed him with warm applause.

As Amir walked onto the stage, the students and parents cheered loudly. I glanced at the Sharma family and my dad, who were seated with bated breath, eager to hear Amir's speech. Ananya and I stood at the corner of the stage, witnessing everything up close. But wait, let me tell you who had the closest view: Vikki Chaturvedi, the chief guest of the event, who was now an MLA. He was probably the happiest person there, seeing his nephew's success.

The anticipation in the air was palpable as Amir approached the podium. His eyes scanned the crowd, and the audience fell silent.

Amir took a deep breath and began his speech.

I am grateful to be here today. I don't want to say much, but there are some things that need to be said.

I see many familiar faces here—some of you who once called me the 'murderer's son.' Well, you're not wrong. It's true. My Abba was a murderer. I'm not saying anyone here is wrong for thinking that. You had your reasons. But that does not define who I am. What the world sees on the surface doesn't capture the whole truth of a person. The perception of our identity is shaped by what society says and we accept it about ourselves. But that's not the end of the story.

When we dig deeper, when we connect to the spiritual essence of who we are, we discover something more powerful. We learn who we truly are and what we are made for. It's in that understanding—of who you are and why you are—that you find your real strength.

That's all I want to leave you with today.

There's one person I want to mention—Vedant Bhaiya. He used to say something that has become a guiding force in my life: 'Live heroically.' His words taught me that no matter what others think, we must rise above it and live with purpose. So, I share them with you now:

Live heroically. Live meaningfully. Die proudly.

And finally, when my time comes, I want to have earned the highest honor—to have my body lifted in the Tiranga, draped in the flag of the nation I have dedicated my life to serve.

Jai Hind.

Epilogue

29 June 2024
India vs South Africa - T20 World Cup Final

We were all packed into the living room of the Sharma house: me, Amir, Ananya, Dadi, Radhika didi, and Raghav. The tension in the air was thick as India's score stood at 34 for 3 in just 4.3 overs. Our hopes were pinned on the screen, each of us silently praying for a miracle.

"Looks like this match will gone," Amir muttered nervously, biting his nails. "There seems to be some bad luck for India in finals."

"Stop being so negative!" Ananya shot back, sitting upright with her arms crossed. "Just wait for Kohli. As long as Kohli is there, anything can happen."

The sound of firecrackers outside from early celebrators added to the chaos, but inside, we all knew it was going to be a tough game. Mr. Sharma, with his much heavier belly than before, walked in with his stethoscope around his neck.

"If India wins today, I'll take care of my patients for free for a week!" he declared with a grin, though his nervous energy was palpable.

What are you saying, Papa!" Radhika didi laughed, nudging him.

Everyone was glued to the TV. Virat Kohli and Axar Patel had just started to stabilize the innings, and the memory of the 2011 World Cup final came rushing back to me.

"Just like Gambhir and Dhoni!" I whispered to Amir. "Yeh Kohli aaj bhi bachayega," Amir nodded.

By the time the innings ended, we had managed a decent total of 176, thanks to Virat Kohli's crucial knock of 76. But South Africa's destructive batting lineup was a real threat.

As the second innings started, the room became even quieter. The atmosphere was heavy with anticipation. When Heinrich Klaasen was on fire, it seemed like the match was slipping away from us.

"This match is going away," Ananya sighed, covering her face with her hands as South Africa needed just 16 runs in the last over. David Miller, their finisher, was on strike.

"Let Hardik Pandya bowl. Watch—something will happen," said Radhika didi.

We all watched in absolute silence as Pandya took his position to bowl the final over. Mr. Sharma's stethoscope clinked nervously against his chest as he moved restlessly in his seat. With 16 runs needed, Miller launched one towards long-off, and the commentator's voice echoed:

"Long off... long off... long off... Suryakumar Yadav!"

Suryakumar Yadav was perfectly placed and made the crucial catch!

"YESSSS!" Amir and I screamed simultaneously, jumping off the couch.

"OUTTTT!" Dadi shouted, laughing, her hands in the air.

The final ball was bowled, and we sealed the victory by 7 runs. India had won the T20 World Cup!

The entire Sharma house erupted. Dadi and I started dancing wildly, and soon Ananya and Amir joined in, their laughter filling the room.

Radhika didi, in the middle of her celebration, suddenly noticed the stethoscope wrapped around Mr. Sharma's neck in the excitement.

"Papa, what's happening!" she laughed, rushing over to help him as he struggled with the stethoscope tangled in his shirt.

The crackers outside had grown even louder, and the chaos in the house matched it. In the middle of the noise, I glanced over to Raghav, sitting awkwardly in the corner, staring at the TV with a serious expression on his face.

"Raghav, come join us!" I called, motioning him over.

Raghav looked at me, his eyes full of determination. "Bhaiya, I want to be there someday," he said quietly. "I want to be like Kohli."

Watching the celebrations continue, I realized that in this moment, just like years ago, another dream was taking root —just like Vedant's had.

I walked over to him and ruffled his hair. "I've got your back. Not just now, but always."